A ROVER'S STORY

New York Times Bestseller
National Indie Bestseller
Washington Post Best Middle Grade Books
Publishers Weekly Best Middle Grade Books
ALA *Booklist* Editors' Choice
ALA Notable Book
Junior Library Guild Selection
Indie Next Selection

"A gripping read. The novel does a terrific job of communicating scientific information to young readers, and it's also emotionally satisfying." —*New York Times Book Review*

"Warga follows her cybernetic narrator from first awareness to final resting place—and stony indeed will be any readers who remain unmoved by the journey. The intelligences here may be (mostly) artificial, but the feelings are genuine and deep." —*Kirkus Reviews* (starred review)

"This touching, fact-filled novel centers the maturation of gutsy Mars rover Resilience." —*Publishers Weekly* (starred review)

"An endlessly inventive story, replete with gentle humor and playful pondering, offering a unique perspective on everything from music and electronics to loyalty and love. A profound and poignant exploration of the universe both outside and within us all." —ALA *Booklist* (starred review)

"Will thrill fans of both adventure and robot stories and also provide intellectual sustenance for the deep thinkers." —*The Horn Book*

"A fresh format and timely topic engage readers in this uplifting and deeply human sci-fi story." —*School Library Journal*

"As a mechanical engineer and STEM-lover, this beautiful book filled my heart right to the top. Res may be a rover, but he taught me what it means to be fully alive."
—Christina Soontornvat, three-time Newbery Honor recipient

THE SHAPE OF THUNDER
Barnes & Noble Children's and YA Book Award Finalist
Boston Globe Best Children's Books
School Library Journal Best Middle Grade Books
Indie Next Selection
Junior Library Guild Selection

"With taut pacing, nuanced characters, and compassionate depictions of grief and trauma, Warga's novel is both timely and transcendent." —*School Library Journal* (starred review)

"Moving and beautifully written, *The Shape of Thunder* is an important book that will push readers to consider what they would do in an impossible situation, and how far they would be willing to go to change it." —*BookPage* (starred review)

"Warga's lyrical language and credible rendering of both middle school life and of the tensions of two families coping differently with personal devastation make for a perceptive, sensitively told novel about the effects of gun violence." —*Publishers Weekly*

"Warga skillfully handles both [a] delicate, emotional friendship and larger subjects of grief and gun violence. Powerful and emotionally complex." —*Kirkus Reviews*

"This will spark meaningful discussions."
—ALA *Booklist*

"Warga skillfully develops unique voices for her narrators. Emotions run high throughout the book without weighing down the plot, and the portrayal of middle-school life is utterly authentic." —*The Horn Book*

A
ROVER'S
STORY

Also by Jasmine Warga

The Shape of Thunder
Other Words for Home
Here We Are Now
My Heart and Other Black Holes

A ROVER'S STORY

JASMINE WARGA

BALZER + BRAY

An Imprint of HarperCollins*Publishers*

Balzer + Bray is an imprint of HarperCollins Publishers.

A Rover's Story
Text copyright © 2022 by Jasmine Warga
Interior art © 2022 by Matt Rockefeller

Library of Congress Cataloging-in-Publication Data

Names: Warga, Jasmine, author.
Title: A rover's story / Jasmine Warga.
Description: First edition. | New York : Balzer + Bray, an imprint of
    HarperCollins Publishers, [2022] | Audience: Ages 8-12. | Audience:
    Grades 4-6. | Summary: Built to explore Mars, Resilience
    begins to develop human-like feelings as he learns from
    the NASA scientists who assembled him, and as he
    blasts off and explores Mars, Resilience must overcome
    different obstacles as he explores the red planet.
Identifiers: LCCN 2022006024 | ISBN 9780063113930 (paperback)
Subjects: CYAC: Roving vehicles (Astronautics)—Fiction. |
    Mars (Planet)—Exploration—Fiction. | LCGFT: Novels.
Classification: LCC PZ7.1.W37 Ro 2022 | DDC [Fic]—dc23
LC record available at https://lccn.loc.gov/2022006024

Typography by Jenna Stempel-Lobell
24 25 26 27 28   PC/CWR   10 9 8 7 6 5 4 3

First paperback edition, 2024

This one's for my mom, who always read to me

PART ONE
PREPARING

THE FIRST DAY

I am not born in the way humans are, but there is a beginning. Beeping. Bright lights. A white room filled with figures in white hazmat suits. So much information to process, but I can handle it. I awake to knowledge. My circuits fire. The room cheers. A loud sound, but it does not startle me.

I am not built for startling. I have been built for observation.

In the sea of unknown figures, I focus on a face.

I do not know if I have a face. If I have one, my information suggests it is not like this one. This face has what humans call lips. The human lips curl upward.

A smile.

I cannot smile—this I know—but somehow I understand the significance of this expression. I am learning.

My mission has begun.

LEARNING

I am built to collect and process information. That is how I learn.

Here is some of the information I have collected:

I am what is referred to as a robot. Most of the other beings around me are called humans. All the humans I interact with wear hazmat suits. This is to prevent microbacteria and dust particles from entering my environment. It is very important for my mission that I am kept in a sterile and clean environment.

For some reason that I do not quite understand yet, humans call the white hazmat suits they wear bunny suits.

I do not know what a bunny is. I frequently wonder about the possibilities.

Most of the humans in bunny suits are what humans term scientists. This, I have deduced, is a subset of human.

Perhaps I am a subset of robot, but I have not encountered enough robots to know for sure.

I will wait to find out. But waiting can be hard.

Dear Rover,

My teacher, Mrs. Ennis, asked us to write a letter to you. She's really excited. She says you're going on an amazing mission where you're going to find out amazing things. Mrs. Ennis really likes the word <u>amazing</u>.

Mrs. Ennis kept looking at me while she talked about you. She even asked me if I wanted to explain to the other kids what you were. And I really didn't. Not at all. No offense, but I'm already sick and tired of hearing about you all the time.

Then she said, "Come on, Sophia." And I didn't want to disappoint Mrs. Ennis, so I told everyone how you are a robot who was created to explore the planet of Mars so that we can understand its atmosphere and environment better. That's kind of a mouthful to say, you know?

I also told them how you were engineered to be really smart and that you are learning new things every day. Like yesterday, Mom told me that your brain learned how to talk to your arm. My classmates had lots of questions, but I didn't know how to answer them. I bet Mom could, though.

Anyway, Mrs. Ennis wants us to enter the contest to name you. I'm not sure I'm going to enter. No offense again. Though if I did enter, I would submit something awesome like: Spicy Sparkle Dragon Blast. I know enough to know that you can't talk like humans do, but if you could, I think you would tell me that you like that name.

Okay, my hand is starting to hurt. I think I've written enough. And anyway, I don't even know if rovers can read. Maybe I'll ask Mom tonight.

Bye!

Sophia

SOMEDAY

One day, all of a sudden, I am taken apart. It is not explained to me why this is happening. It is also not explained to me when or if I will be put together again.

I would really like to be put together again.

"Hello?" I say. "Please put me back together."

No one responds. No one explains why this is happening.

Once I am disassembled, I am left with only my brain—a computer sitting still, suspended on a long laboratory table. My cameras are gone so my vision is gone, too. I am only able to sense and observe things through hearing.

I listen as the hazmats move around me, running tests on all my different body parts. Through these tests, I begin to better understand what is going on.

Code is transmitted to my brain. And I welcome the communication.

The code I receive asks me to do different things such as move the part of my body the hazmats call my arm. My arm is no longer physically connected to me, but my brain is still able to control and monitor its movement.

I understand when a test goes well. And I understand when a test fails. I do this by reading the code.

Of all the tests, the ones run on my cameras are my

favorite. Because when my cameras are on, I can once again visually process my surroundings.

I can see.

When my cameras are not being tested, there is only darkness.

The darkness is an unfavorable condition for me. I do not like it at all.

I have heard the hazmats refer to my cameras as my eyes. I do not know if this is an accurate term, but I have stored it to my memory. It is a term that I like because it makes me feel similar to the hazmats. And being a hazmat seems like a wonderful thing to be.

The hazmats are not in pieces. All of their parts have been put together. The hazmats are able to move around as they please. The hazmats are able to talk with one another.

And the hazmats are never left alone in darkness. Unable to move. Have I mentioned that I am unable to move?

When I sit, suspended on the table, in the darkness, my brain cycles through many thoughts. Most of them are not enjoyable.

But there is one enjoyable thought. This thought arises from listening to the hazmats. From information I have overheard, I have developed an understanding that someday, perhaps someday soon, I will be put together again.

I like to think about this. It is a good thought. It is a good thought because it means someday I will be whole again. Which means that someday I will be able to move. And best of all, someday, I will be able to use my cameras at all times to see.

I do not have the information that tells me when someday is. When someday will be. All I can do is wait. And listen.

So I wait. And I listen.

But waiting is hard.

I am starting to think that I was not built for waiting.

RANIA

There is a large team of scientists who work with me. Humans would tell you that it is impossible for me to have a preference. That I am built to be an unbiased observer. Perhaps, though, there is a flaw in my code, because I have some favorites among the hazmats.

The first of which is Rania.

Rania is in charge of running many of my tests. She writes the code that asks my arm to bend down and pick up an object. She writes code to ask if I am able to see that she is testing my arm. It is nice to talk to Rania in this way, through code.

Once, when Rania was running a test on my camera, I was able to see her. Beneath her white hazmat suit, I observed that she has light brown skin and hair with pigments of black and brown. Her eyes share similar pigments to her hair. I have memorized that image. I now associate that image with the sounds that Rania makes in the laboratory.

Rania never calls her hazmat suit a bunny suit. Rania refers to everything by its correct terminology. I appreciate this precision.

Rania is often the first figure I observe when the day begins, and often the last of the hazmats to leave the laboratory at night. Most of the time, I cannot visually process Rania since my camera—my eyes—are not currently connected to my brain.

But I am still able to perceive her. My brain is able to make other observations like sound and registering of presence to know that Rania is there.

Rania has a very noticeable presence.

Her behavior follows a clear pattern. Rania is rhythm and dependability. Rania is the sound of typing computer keys and measured answers full of exact calculations. Rania is elegantly written code without any of the problems that hazmats call bugs.

When Rania speaks in the language of humans, her voice is crisp and clear. Rania never talks directly to me in her clear and crisp voice, but I like listening to her talk to the other hazmats. She almost always has the answers they are looking for. When she does not, she promises to get back to them as soon as possible.

*As soon as possibl*e is a phrase I have learned from Rania. I am hoping that all my different body parts will be put together as soon as possible. Unfortunately, I am not able to express this message to Rania because I am unable to talk in the language of humans.

Rania only speaks to me through code. And I can only

answer her in code, and only to answer the specific questions that she asks, like *Can you tell I'm testing your arm?*

I am able to say yes or no. I am not able to ask her a question about her day. I am not able to ask her when my body parts will be welded back together. I am not able to tell her that waiting is hard.

I do not have the ability of human speech. It seems unlikely that I will ever have the ability of human speech. This is a fact that frustrates me sometimes.

Frustrate is another word I have learned from Rania. Sometimes when she is alone in the lab, she speaks into her phone. She says things to her phone like "Mama, I know you are frustrated that I'm going to miss dinner again, but the work I am doing here is really important."

It made me feel important to hear Rania say that. It also made me forget about my frustration that I can't talk directly to Rania. And my frustration that I'm still in pieces.

At least it made me forget for a little. I would still like to be put together as soon as possible.

Dear Rover,

Mrs. Ennis hasn't told us to write you again, but I'm writing anyway. I don't know why. I guess I was feeling like I wanted to talk to someone.

Tonight at dinner, I asked Mom if rovers could read. She told me that's a "great question" that has "lots of different answers," which is a very Mom thing to say. Sitti told Mom to "just give Sophia a straight answer!" Which made me laugh. Sitti is my grandma. I call her Sitti because that's the Arabic word for grandma.

After dinner, Mom went back to work. Does she talk to you when she's there? What does she say?

Sometimes I struggle to fall asleep when Mom isn't here. Once in a while, Sitti will come into my room and sing me a song. Occasionally, Dad sneaks in and tells me a story about a giant that lives in the mountains or a cursed kingdom that gets saved by a brave princess. Dad always has the best stories. But no matter how good the story is, it's still hard to get to sleep when I know Mom is gone.

11

So maybe that's why I'm writing you now. Because I miss Mom. And I know you're with her. Say hi to her for me? I wonder how you say hi in robot. Maybe someday you can teach me.

Your sleepy friend (can I call you my friend?),

Sophia

XANDER

Another scientist I have developed a preference for is named Xander. Xander works with Rania. When Xander ran a test on one of my cameras, I observed that he has pale white skin, gray eyes, and hair that my system identifies as having both red and brown pigments.

Xander is always moving. He frequently paces around the lab. Xander likes to call his hazmat suit a bunny suit. He also likes to make what humans call jokes. Sometimes I understand the humor; sometimes I don't. It doesn't bother me too much when I don't understand, though, because Rania hardly ever seems to get Xander's jokes either.

"Why didn't the tree like checkers?" Xander says to Rania while she is checking the code that will help me to steer once I am connected to my wheels again.

"I don't know what you're saying," Rania answers.

"Because it was a chestnut!"

Xander laughs and Rania does not.

"Get it?" Xander says.

Rania does not reply. She keeps typing.

But even though I frequently do not understand Xander's humor, I like him very much. I feel quite . . . connected to him.

Perhaps this is because Xander is the one who informs me of my name. We are all alone when he tells me. No one else is in the room. Not even Rania.

"A sixth grader in Ohio wrote this," he says. Even though I can't visually see him, I detect that he is reading off a tablet. Almost all the hazmat suit humans carry tablets.

Tablets, I have come to understand, are small computers. I sometimes try to talk to the tablets. I have recently discovered that I am able to talk to other machines. Rania's phone is quite chatty. The tablets, though, are not great conversationalists. They are very focused on productivity.

"Let me read you what the sixth grader wrote in her essay. It's wonderful," Xander says.

I do not know what a sixth grader is. I do not know what Ohio is. But both words seem important. I store them in my system.

Xander walks, his footsteps making an echoing sound. He clears his throat and reads off his tablet. "'My name is Cadence and I think you should name the new Mars Rover Resilience. *Resilience* is a noun that means the power or ability to return to the original form after being bent, compressed, or stretched. It can also mean elasticity. There is another definition in which resilience means the ability to recover easily for adversity. The dictionary also says resilience can mean buoyancy, which is the ability to float.

"'My science teacher told us that this Mars Rover has

a big task. It is going to collect samples from the surface of Mars, explore the terrain and photograph it, as well as try to bring back online another Mars Rover who NASA lost connection with. To me, that sounds like a job that will need resilience. This rover will need to be able to stay afloat even when things are difficult. I have read that the landing can be especially tricky. I think having a name that can mean "to float" will be good luck for the tricky landing.

"'There will probably be lots of setbacks, but this rover will hopefully adapt. That is why I think you should name this Mars Rover Resilience.'

"Isn't that an awesome essay, buddy?" Xander says.

I observe that he is using *buddy* to refer to me.

That means I am Xander's buddy. And Xander is my buddy. I register this.

"So many people wrote to us, but out of all the essays, this is the one that was chosen as the winner. Your name is Resilience. But I think I'm going to call you Res for short. What do you think . . . ?" He pauses for a second and then adds, "Res?"

He laughs. Maybe this is another one of his jokes. I am not sure what is funny, but I like the sound of his laugh. He touches the main computer part of my body, my brain, with his gloved hand. I can sense it somehow, even though I can't see it. Perhaps the right way to phrase this sensation would be to say, I feel it.

I am a Mars Rover. My name is Resilience. My nickname is Res. You are given a nickname when you have a buddy.

I am Xander's buddy.

I can feel it.

JOURNEY

There is another Mars Rover. One that is almost exactly like me.

I learn of this Mars Rover the day my cameras are connected to my brain. My entire body is still not whole—the scientists have not yet assembled my wheels or my arm or installed my outer shell.

But the cameras are a big first step. I am able to see all around me now, not just sense the presence of objects. And in all this seeing, I spot the other rover. She is in the room next to mine. I can see her through the glass-windowed wall that separates us. She is like me, but different.

She is not in pieces. Her brain is connected to her body, which is connected to her arm and to her camera eyes and to her wheels.

"You and this Rover are the same. Identical. You are like siblings," Xander tells me. He points at the rover through the glass window.

"Siblings? No," Rania says. "Stop anthropomorphizing. It's not professional."

"Ignore her, Res. She's just jealous of our relationship," Xander says.

"It is so weird that you talk to the rover," Rania says.

"When you type code for it, you are talking to it."

"That's different," Rania says.

I like Rania's code. I always understand what she is asking me to do. The tasks are clear, like lift your arm or take a photograph with your third rear left-side camera or turn your wheels to the right.

But I also like that Xander talks to me using human speech. It is frustrating that I cannot talk back. I understand what he is saying, though. And I have a strong feeling that Xander somehow knows this.

Once, when we were all in the lab, Rania said to Xander, "Trust me." She was editing his code. "This will work," she said.

And she was right. It worked. My wheels spun when she asked them to.

Trust me. That's what Rania had said.

Trust. Me.

Trust was a word that I stored in my system. At first, I did not know what it meant. Humans have many words for their many feelings. From listening to the hazmats talk (especially from listening to Rania when she is on her phone), I have mastered an understanding of sad and happy and angry and proud and, of course, frustrated. But trust has been hard to learn. Recently, though, I am fairly sure I have figured it out.

Trust is what Xander has for me and my understanding of human speech. Trust is what Xander has when he lets Rania rewrite his code. Trust is what Rania has in our mission when she cancels her dinner plans with her family once again to stay late to work.

It is a good thing to be trusted. Trust is something that the hazmats value. And so I am learning to value it, too.

I would like to be able to tell Xander that I trust him. And also to tell Rania that I trust her. That I trust her code more than anything.

I suppose that is another thing I have recently developed along with my preferences—the ability to want things to happen. Sometimes I think this might disappoint Rania if she knew this about me since she does not like when Xander acts as if I am capable of human feelings. I would never want to disappoint Rania. I would never want to give her a reason to not trust in our mission.

"That is Journey," Xander says. He points at the rover again. Rania doesn't say anything, but she looks in the direction of Xander's finger.

Once I am whole, I will look exactly like Journey. Journey already has her six wheels. We each will have a chemistry lab built inside our bodies so that we will be able to collect samples from Mars's soil and analyze it. We each will have a working arm that we can use to collect those samples.

Journey already has her working arm. I think the human

word for the feeling I have about that is jealous. If I had the ability of human speech, I would ask Xander why Journey already has her arm. I would ask if it is because she is a better rover than me.

But I cannot ask Xander and Rania those questions. Instead, I go back to observing Journey. From studying her, I can learn more about my future body.

"Hello," Journey says through the glass wall. That is one of the benefits of machine-speak. Glass walls are no barrier.

"Hello," I answer.

TALKING

The hazmats do not hear us when me and Journey talk. It is a form of language at a frequency that they cannot hear and do not understand. The hazmats seem to have an awareness of everything that happens in the lab, but it is unclear whether they know that Journey and I talk to one another.

Sometimes I like the idea that they do not know. That it is something only for Journey and me.

"Why do you call them hazmats?" Journey asks me.

"Because they wear hazmats," I say.

"They refer to the hazmats as bunny suits."

"I know."

"They are humans."

"I know."

"They are scientists."

"You should be specific," Journey says.

"I am. *Hazmat* is specific. It is a subset of humans that are scientists that wear hazmat suits. I have sorted and defined it."

"Hazmat is an abbreviation for hazardous material," Journey says.

I did not know this. I do not tell Journey, though. I had

picked up the term *hazmat* from my environment. I had not searched for more information. This was a failing, but I have overcome it. I store this new information from Journey in my system. I will not make the same mistake again.

Even though Journey often corrects me, I still enjoy talking with her. It is different than communicating with Rania and Xander. When I tell Journey this, she says, "Beeps and boops, *enjoy* is not a concept in our programming."

But I have heard Xander use the word *enjoy*. And I am Xander's buddy.

"Why are you called Journey?" I ask.

"I do not know," Journey says.

I observe that maybe Journey needs a buddy, too.

BACKUP

"You are whole," I say. With the cameras attached, I am no longer just a brain sitting on a table in the laboratory. Now I am a brain with twenty-three cameras attached to it sitting on a table in a laboratory. Once in a while, the hazmats remove one of those cameras to test it. But twenty-three cameras gives you access to a lot of visuals. Even when one is missing, I can still see plenty.

Journey also has her twenty-three cameras. And her wheels. Plus, Journey gets to move around the laboratory. She is always being asked to move. Getting to climb up and over obstacles that the hazmats lay out in the laboratory.

I have a human feeling that I don't like when she tells me about these tests.

"I am not whole yet," I say.

"Perhaps you are a backup," she tells me.

"A backup?"

"That is the term humans use to refer to a duplicate copy of a machine. It appears you are a duplicate of me. If I fail, you will be needed."

"I think we both are needed."

"Beeps and boops, that does not appear to be a statement based in fact," Journey says.

"Where did you learn the term *beeps* and *boops*?"

Journey is quiet for a moment. It is not like her to be quiet. She is a fast processor. Her answers normally come at rapid speed.

"Journey?" I say.

"I created it."

"You created it?"

"It is my phrase."

"Oh," I say.

"Do you think that is unscientific?"

"No," I say without a pause. "I think it is extraordinary."

It has never occurred to me that I could create a phrase. That I could create anything. I have spent all my time observing. Learning everything that I possibly could. But never creating.

"It came to me one day," Journey adds.

I can't stop thinking about the fact that Journey created something new. I also cannot stop thinking about the idea that I am a backup. This new information brings about a variety of human feelings. Some are good. And some are bad. Human feelings can be confusing in that way. They are not always easy to sort out.

"Wait," I say.

"What should I wait for?"

Wait is something I have heard Xander say to Rania when he is asking for time. Rania is usually faster than Xander when it comes to solving problems.

"That is an expression," I say.

"You did not create it."

"No," I say. "But I observed it."

"Beeps and boops, what am I waiting for?"

"Do you really think I'm a backup?"

"I'm waiting for that?" Journey says.

"It was an expression to ask you to return to a previous topic. And that topic was that of whether or not I am a backup robot."

"Oh," Journey says. "I am not certain. But it is quite likely you are a backup. I would put the odds at approximately seventy-two point five percent."

"That is a ridiculous probability. I do not think there is much accuracy to it," I say. I do not know if my statement is right, but I very much want it to be.

"I disagree. Based on the facts I currently have, I would say it is exceedingly accurate."

"You're wrong," I say. "I am going to Mars."

"How do you know?"

"I just do."

"That's very unscientific reasoning," Journey says, and I can tell that she doesn't believe me. That she is still viewing me as a backup.

But I'm not a backup. I can't be. I was built to go to Mars.

"I'm seventy-two point five percent certain I'm going to Mars," I finally say. It sounds like something Xander would say. I think I say it for that reason.

"Beeps and boops," says Journey.

Dear Resilience,

I can use your name now! They finally announced the winner of the contest. She is a girl named Cadence and she lives in Ohio and she is in sixth grade like me. I mean, Resilience is a pretty good name. I'll admit that. But Spicy Sparkle Dragon Blast would've been AWESOME.

Mom laughed so hard when I told her that was the name I submitted. (Fine—I did enter the contest. I couldn't resist.) She spit up some water, which made her laugh even harder. It is hard to make Mom laugh, so I felt pretty proud of myself. You know what else Mom told me? That everyone in the lab calls you Res for short.

I considered telling Mrs. Ennis about your nickname so that she could tell our class, but I'm keeping it a secret for now. I like that it's something only I know. Well, and everyone else who works at the lab. But you know what I mean, I think. Mom says that you're really smart.

I feel like I know so much about you and you don't really know a lot about me. So here are some important things

27

you should know: my favorite color is aquamarine, I play soccer and my position is midfielder, and I've seen the movie *Moana* about five hundred times. Do you know what movies are? Mom says you'll make movies when you get to Mars. I told her I wasn't sure I'd want to watch them, which I know was mean, but I was feeling grumpy that she was going to be working late again.

The truth is, I'll definitely watch your movies.

Your friend,

Sophie (my full name is Sophia but my friends all call me Sophie, and I feel like you should too!)

ENVIRONMENTS

I don't see Journey as much as I see Xander and Rania. Journey gets to move all over the laboratory. Journey gets to participate in what the hazmats call "field tests." But I am still stuck in this one room, suspended on this one table.

Journey and I work with separate teams. I wonder what Journey calls her team. She probably uses another word. That makes sense. We have observed different things.

Journey has not observed the look in Rania's eyes. She has not heard Rania talk on the phone to her mom. She has not listened to the humming sound Rania makes when she is typing code. She has not heard Rania mumble to herself, "This better work" or "This better be worth it."

When you hear a hazmat say that over and over again, you decide to want to be worth it. Even if you aren't quite sure what that means.

Journey has not heard Xander's laugh, deep and textured. Journey has not listened to Xander read aloud from a sixth grader named Cadence's essay. Journey does not know why she is called Journey.

Our environments have been different.

Environments matter.

I think if I said that to Journey, she would say, "Beeps and boops."

But environments do matter. Beeps and boops.

SUCCESSFUL

From listening to the hazmats, I know I am not the first of my kind.

I am not the second of my kind either. There have been many Mars Rovers.

Some of those rovers have been what the hazmats call "successful." Some have not. The nots crashed into the surface of Mars during landing, which means they never got the chance to explore. Or the nots got permanently stuck when their mission had just begun, their wheels thwarted by particularly rocky soil. Or their interior computer brain went completely buggy and they were no longer able to communicate with Earth. That last one sounds particularly bad.

I would not like to experience that.

Rania and Xander and the other hazmats very much want Journey and me to be "successful." It is easy for me to understand what has made a rover not successful. It is not as easy, though, for me to understand what makes one successful. But I want to figure it out.

When I tell all of this to Journey, Journey says, "Beeps and boops. Want is not in our programming."

But want is in my programming. I am sure of it. Because I do want.

I watch Rania's eyes as she runs the numbers, as she goes through calculation after calculation. Rania and Xander are the most concerned about the part of the mission that they call the landing. This is when I will fall from space onto Mars's surface. This is the part where I am most likely to crash, where I am most likely to be unsuccessful.

Rania has started staying later and later at night. I listen to her phone calls with her mother. I have learned that when Rania talks to her mother, she speaks in a language the hazmats call Arabic. This is different from the language of English, which is the language she speaks in with Xander. All human languages take place at the same pitch and frequency, which makes them sound similar to me as I translate them for my own understanding.

Rania only talks to her mother when all the other hazmats have left the laboratory, when she is the last one here.

"Mama, I know," Rania says. "Yes, of course, I would love to be there right now, but I just can't. Can you put her on the phone?"

I do not know who *her* is. And I do not know the precise meaning of this word that she used—*love*. But Rania's voice changes when she switches from talking to her mom to talking to this unknown *her*. Her voice is less crisp, more fuzzy.

Hearing her voice sound like this gives me a good feeling, a human emotion I am not sure I have the name for yet.

"Twinkle, twinkle, little star," Rania sings into the phone. I hear a tiny voice sing back. I have never sung before. But I would like to learn how.

"Good night, Sophie," Rania says.

That is how I learn that Sophie is *her*. Based on Rania's tone of voice, I am able to easily observe that Sophie is very important to Rania.

I listen to many phone calls between Rania and Sophie, between Rania and her mother.

During another phone call with her mother, Rania says, "Mama, I'm sorry. I just can't. We're getting closer and closer to launch. Mama, you're not listening to me."

And another: "Yes, it's important. This has been over seven years of my life, Mama—I can't give up now." Rania makes a loud snorting sound. "Yeah, yeah, I hope it'll be worth it too."

After Rania hangs up from that phone call, she looks right at me. I really think she might talk to me in human speech for the first time. I want so badly to say, *I'm going to try to be worth it. Trust me, Rania.*

But she doesn't talk to me. And I can't talk to her.

I am only able to sit on the table and wait.

LANDINGS

The landing is often the most difficult part of the mission. The hazmats frequently call the landing "The Seven Minutes of Terror." Terror is not something I am sure I can experience. But it does not sound pleasant. It would be preferable to avoid it, if possible.

From listening to the hazmats talk, I have deciphered that during those seven minutes, Journey and I will be on our own. We will be in full control of steering and guiding our own landing. This is because it takes too long to get a message from Earth to Mars. Therefore, the hazmats have to trust us to complete the landing on our own.

During the landing, I will have to prove that I am worthy of that trust.

Rania spends a lot of time running numbers and simulations about how I will land. She does this late at night. She does this even when her mother and Sophie and Scott really want her to come home. Scott, I have learned, is what the hazmats call a husband. He seems very important to Rania, too.

One night, I hear Rania talking to Sophie. She has already sung "Twinkle, Twinkle." "Soph," Rania says. "I know it is hard to wait. But I promise I'm going to be home soon. The time will go faster if you get to sleep."

Sophie, I realize, is like me. She does not like to wait.

"Good night, lovebug. I love you to the moon and back," Rania says in her fuzzy voice—the voice she only uses when she talks to Sophie—and hangs up the phone. She goes back to trying to figure out the calculations to ensure that I have a safe landing.

Even if Journey says want is not in our programming, I want to land.

I do not want to crash.

Want. Want. Want. This is a human feeling I have grown very familiar with.

A rover who is worth it will not crash.

I don't want to crash.

RANIA'S PHONE

I cannot talk in human speech to Rania, but I can talk in machine speech to her phone. Her phone is not that interested in talking to me, though. The phone seems to like to play games all day when she is not in use.

"Do you have a name?" I say.

"I am busy. Level 33."

"That is your name? I am busy, Level 33."

"No, I am busy. Level 33."

"Okay," I say, still not sure I am processing the information correctly. "I am worried about Rania."

"Worried? You're worried? *Worried* is not a word for you. Worried is a word for her mother. Her mother uses worried all the time."

"That's why I'm worried. I hear those conversations," I say.

"Oh, YOU hear those conversations? Try being me. I AM those conversations. Dang! I received a text message, and I got distracted. Game over. Time to start again."

"Game over?"

"I lost at Level 33."

"Do you think Rania is okay?"

"I do not know how to answer that."

"Her mother seems worried about her."

"Yes. Her mother is worried."

"Why?" I ask.

"She works a lot. All the time. Her mother is worried that Rania is giving up too much of her life for her work, for you. Zing! Level 2. Here we go. We are rolling."

"Giving up too much for me?"

"That she is missing out on time with her family. Rania really misses Scott and Sophie and her mother when she is here at work. Missing out on her life, you know what I'm saying? Case in point, she downloaded this game three years ago but hasn't played it once. It's a great game, too. I play it all the time. Anyway, Rania misses lots of family things. Like special dinners and Sophie's soccer games. I see her put those events on her calendar, but she never goes to them. Man, those phone calls with her mother all start to sound the same. Wah, wah, wah, so boring. Hooray! Zing again! Moving on to Level 3. Also, how many times can we listen to that one song?"

"'Twinkle, Twinkle'?" I ask. "It is a beautiful song." *Beautiful* is a word I have learned from the hazmats. It is a word that sounds like what it means. It is a word that sounds like Rania's voice when she sings to Sophie.

"Not sure I agree. Ugh! Oh, wait. Yay! Made it to Level 4."

"I'm going to be worth it," I tell Rania's phone. "All the things she missed, it will be okay because I'm going to do an amazing job on Mars."

"Okay, Rover. Whatever you say."

"My name is Resilience," I say. The phone doesn't respond after that, but it still feels good to have said it.

Dear Res,

Is it okay if I call you Res? Mom says that is what everyone at the lab calls you. And it's easier for me to spell than Resilience.

I scored three goals at my soccer game yesterday. Mom wasn't there to see it. You know why? Because she was working on you. You sure take up a lot of time. Dad and Sitti cheered extra loud for my goals, but I still missed hearing Mom shout.

Sometimes I get mad at you. But the real truth, which is hard to say, is that I'm kind of mad at Mom. Even though I'm proud of her, too. Dad says Mom and everyone else at Jet Propulsion Laboratory and NASA are changing the world. That might be true, but I still would've really liked her to watch me score.

Mom, Dad, and I went out for ice cream on Sunday because Mom felt bad about missing my soccer game. She showed me pictures of your brain. No offense, but you look sort of funny.

Does your brain make it so you can be lonely? Like when Mom goes home, and you are left all by yourself, do you feel lonely? I feel lonely right now.

Mom says I might get to come to the lab soon to meet you. I think that would be really cool. I know you can't actually talk, but I still would like to say hi. I bet you'd understand.

Okay, I'm going to try to go to sleep now. I know rovers don't sleep, but I'm a human, so I have to.

Your friend,

Sophie

WHOLE

Today I am built.

All my pieces connected. Whole.

"Looking good, Res," Xander says.

Rania rolls her eyes, but she smiles a little. I can tell she thinks I'm looking good, too.

Each of my body parts is able to talk to one another. Or more accurately, my brain is able to talk to all my body parts.

"Look," I tell Journey that night. "I am built."

"You still haven't moved."

"But I could."

That is not entirely accurate. Right now, I have code that prevents me from moving on my own. But I can feel the possibility of movement in my wheels.

"See," I say. "I am not a backup."

"You don't know that. It is possible they are building you to test you as a backup."

"I am going to Mars."

"There is no way for you to be certain of that," Journey says.

"Wait. Are you certain of it?" I ask.

"You are frequently asking me to wait."

"Wait is like my beeps and boops."

"Beeps and boops, it is not. You did not make it up."

"Okay," I say. There is silence for a long time, only the hum of the industrial fan overhead. Then I say, "How are you so certain that you are going to Mars?"

"We were built for a mission to Mars."

"Yes," I say. "*We* were. We're going to Mars together."

"Beeps and boops, but yes, by my calculations, that appears to be the most probable outcome."

I don't let that beeps and boops distract me from the fact Journey said she thinks it is probable that I am going to Mars! This makes me feel one of the very best human feelings.

"I am glad to be going with you. We're going to discover great things."

"Glad? You sound like a human."

I am not sure what to say. "I am learning lots of things from the hazmats. Aren't you?"

"I am not learning human feelings. We are not supposed to learn human feelings. Human feelings will not serve us well on Mars."

I do not know if Journey is right. But if she is right, I need to stop learning human feelings. The most important thing is that I do a good job on our mission.

I think of Rania's late-night phone calls with her mother.

I think of the way her voice gets fuzzy when she talks to Sophie, of how softly and gently she sings "Twinkle, Twinkle." I think of the way she says, "I hope it's worth it, too."

"But you think I'm going to get to go, right?" I ask.

"Resilience," Journey says. "I do not have a way of knowing that for certain. And it is not in my programming to make guesses based on information I do not have."

It is the first time Journey has called me by my name. I try to resist having a human feeling about that. My resistance, though, proves to be futile. The human emotion stays. It is another great one.

"You gave me the probability before."

"That was a mistake," Journey says. "It will not happen again."

There is the slow hiss of the air filters. And the ceiling fan still drones on, a soft hum. A hazmat must have left the fan on for the night. Other than those, I do not detect any other sounds. I wait in the quiet for Journey to continue our conversation.

"You do understand that the hazmats built us to be different from them, right?" Journey says, finally breaking the silence.

"Yes," I say, even though for one of the first times I am not sure I actually understand. I usually understand everything. It is a confusing and terrible feeling to not understand something.

"We are built to be logical. To make calculated decisions. You could say that is the opposite of human feelings."

"Why?"

"Beeps and boops, what do you mean why?"

"Why would human feelings be bad on Mars?"

"Are you making a humanlike joke?"

"No. I am being very serious," I say.

"Resilience, don't you understand that human feelings are dangerous? They make humans make poor decisions. You see, humans have attachments. They care about each other and about other things here on Earth. And because of their attachments and their feelings, they do things that are dangerous. We were built to avoid the problems of humans. We were built to make good decisions."

Overhead, the lights flash on. This is a sign that the hazmats are returning. That it is the time of day they call morning. Slowly, and then all at once, the lab fills up with the sounds of human footsteps and human voices.

"On Mars, I will make good decisions," I say.

"Okay," Journey says.

"I really will," I say to Journey.

I will be a rover who is worth it.

Dear Res,

Mom showed me more pictures of you. This time
you looked different. You weren't just your brain.
You actually look pretty cute. I didn't tell Mom that,
though.

When Mom isn't around, I ask Dad and Sitti a lot of
questions about you. Dad says I should tell Mom that I'm
interested in you and that would make her happy. When
Dad said that, Sitti made this clucking noise with her
tongue.

Later that night, I went upstairs and looked at NASA's
website to learn more about you. They have this cool
chart that explains all the different parts of your body.
I discovered that you don't just have one brain—you have
two. That's so you have a backup brain in case something
goes wrong with the first. That's lucky. Humans don't get
backup brains.

I also learned that while my brain is protected by my
skull, your brain is protected by something called a

warm electronics box. My mom and everyone else who works at JPL call it a WEB. I don't know why Mom and the other scientists love abbreviations so much. But all your electronics like your cameras and your brain are stored inside the WEB to keep them safe.

WEB makes me think of a spider. But you aren't a spider. You're a robot.

I know you don't eat food, which I think is kind of sad because that means you'll never taste chocolate chips (which are like the world's greatest food), but NASA's website says you do have something that gives you a sense similar to taste and smell. That's your chemical and mineral sensor. And you also have your arm, which is how you'll collect the chemical and minerals.

The thing everyone seems most excited about is your microphone. Did you know you are the first rover who is getting a microphone? That means you are going to actually be able to record what it sounds like on Mars. What do you think you'll hear?

Anyway, I thought I would get bored reading so much about you, but once I started, I couldn't stop. I know a ton now. I'll probably tell Mom at some point, but I feel like she'll do that thing where she gets overexcited and it's just embarrassing for everyone.

Your friend,

Sophie

ROVE

I am wheeled into a room I have never been in before. It looks like a larger version of the laboratory where I have spent my entire existence. Tiled floor. Bright fluorescent lights. White walls. I am placed in the corner of the new room.

The room is crowded with hazmats. Many of them are holding up their tablets. Some of them are holding up their phones. The phones and the tablets talk to me.

"Good luck, rover!" they say.

"Thank you," I say, and then I add, "I have a name. It is Resilience."

"Good luck, rover!" they still say. Oh well.

"It's showtime, buddy," Xander says.

Then I receive a code message. It is from Rania. I know it is from Rania because her code is clearer than any other hazmat's code. It does not have any bugs. The code tells me to move.

So I move.

When I move, it is called roving.

I move slowly. I do not go far.

But I move.

And the room erupts with hazmat screaming and yelling.

I think it is the happy kind of screaming and yelling. The kind hazmats call cheering.

"Wow!" Xander shouts. "Wow, wow, wow! Hooray!"

All the hazmats are making high-pitched sounds. They are clicking their phones and tablets. Even Rania, who is always calm, has her hands in the air.

The phones and tablets say, "Good job, rover!"

"My name is Resilience," I say again. More for me than for them.

I wonder if I should move my own arm up.

I don't. It isn't in my code.

But I do feel a human feeling inside my system. If I were to give the feeling a sound, it would sound like the hazmats' cheering. It would sound like Xander saying the word *wow*.

Wow.

FAMILY

"There is someone I want you to meet," Xander tells me. He is standing with another hazmat I have never seen before.

This hazmat is shorter in height than Xander, but my system tells me that their hair shares the same color pigments. Their eyes are also similar. There is a pattern of relation. My system connects this information.

"This is my sister, Aria," Xander says.

Sister. This is not a word I know. I search my knowledge base but come up blank. I wonder if sister is like buddy. Xander is smiling when he says the word. This makes me think that sister is a good thing to be.

"Can I take a picture?" the hazmat named Aria says.

"Of course!" Xander says. "He would love that. Wouldn't you, Res?"

Aria presses a button on her phone. Underneath her hazmat, I see her smile. Xander is smiling, too. Their smiles are alike. Another pattern of relation.

I want to smile. I really would like to learn how. I would like for Xander to know that I am happy. That I can be happy. That this is a human emotion I understand.

But then I think about what Journey said about human

emotions being dangerous on a mission to Mars. I guess it is maybe a good thing that I was not built to smile. That way I can keep my human emotions a secret. But it does not feel so good to keep secrets from the hazmats. Human emotions are so very confusing.

"Hey, Mom! I want a photo, too!"

A small hazmat runs toward me. Rania chases after her. "Lovebug, be careful. You don't want to knock into someone."

Lovebug. I have heard that name before. It is a name that Rania has said into the phone many times.

When the small hazmat reaches me, she is smiling wide. I detect that she looks like a lot like Rania. They both have light brown skin and dark hair with pigments of brown and black.

"Hello," I say, even though I know she will not be able to understand me.

The small hazmat hands Rania her phone. "Will you take a photo of me and Res?"

She knows my name! Inside my system, the human emotion of happy grows and grows.

"Sure, lovebug," Rania says.

"Hey," another hazmat says. "Sophie, why don't I take a photo of you and Mom with the rover?"

Sophie and Lovebug are the same. My computer brain makes this connection. I decide I will think of Sophie as Lovebug.

Underneath Lovebug's face shield, I see her crinkle together her eyebrows and wrinkle her nose. "But I want a photo of just me to show everyone."

"It's okay, Scott," Rania says, and Rania takes the photo.

"Okay," Lovebug says. "Now I want one with Mom."

This makes Rania smile very wide, wider than I have ever seen her smile before, and I am not sure I have ever felt this much of the human emotion of happy.

I repeat aloud to myself what I heard Xander say earlier, "Wow."

THE SHAKE AND BAKE

Today is the Shake and Bake test. All the hazmat suits have been talking about it. There is a new look in Rania's eyes, but I am not sure what it means.

Before the test begins, I am carted into a room I've never seen before.

The doors shut. I am alone.

Suddenly, I am shaking. I am turning over. My wheels are spinning faster than ever. Two of my six wheels pull up off the ground.

I am unstable.

Eventually, my wheels find footing again, but the shaking continues. Up and down. Back and forth. Over and over again.

I do not know what is happening, but I do not like it at all.

My system is overloading. I can tell I will shut down soon—

It all stops.

The door opens again.

The hazmat figures return. I search for Rania. I search for Xander.

When I find Rania, there is another look in her eyes. Her eyes are softer, less sharp. I think it is a good look. I store it in my system so I can remember it.

"Good job, Res," Xander says.

Dear Res,

I can't believe I finally got to meet you!!

I love the picture of us! I've shown it to all my friends.
And I showed it to Mrs. Ennis, who, of course, said it was
AMAZING. But it really is pretty amazing. I especially like the
photo of Mom, me, and you, but I didn't show anyone that
one. I've kept it to myself.

Tonight, Mom made it home for dinner. She was in such a
good mood that she let us grab cheeseburgers from my
favorite place, and Sitti didn't even complain, and Sitti
ALWAYS complains when we get cheeseburgers.

I think Mom was in such a good mood because you passed
your Shake and Bake test. Congratulations! I know it was a
big test. I always feel really nervous before tests, like my
stomach is going to erupt. Can rovers vomit? I don't think
so. Anyways, you didn't vomit! You did amazing!

Ugh. Speaking of nervous, I feel a little nervous about you
leaving for Mars. Like I know you'll do a good job, but it
just seems kind of scary.

Tonight it's been hard to get to sleep—not because I miss Mom for once, but because I'm kind of worried I'll miss you when you go. That's silly, right? Yeah. It's silly.

Your friend,

Sophie

MORE TESTS

In the next few days, there are so many hazmat hands. They reach inside my body. They adjust things. They fidget with my cameras. They rewire the way my brain is connected to my body. They check the security bolts on my wheels. They check and check and check.

I am wheeled into a room where I am subjected to freezing temperatures. The temperature is so low that I think I will most certainly go offline, but amazingly, I do not.

Then I am pushed into another room that is as hot as the other room was cold. I hear one of the hazmat suits use the word *scorching*. I save that word. I process it.

The room *is* scorching—the heat burns on the sides of my outer shell—but I withstand it.

It is clear to me that they are looking for something that is wrong. Every day, they search. And every day, at the end of the day, I look at Rania's eyes. When I find the good look, I know I have passed the test. That we are one step closer to the mission being a success. To the mission being worth it.

I almost always find the good look. Once, I think I saw something different. But it vanished as quickly as it appeared. I try not to worry about it too much, though.

EVEN MORE TESTS.
EVEN MORE INFORMATION.

More tests are run. I pass every single one.

Xander says, "Good job, Res."

Journey does other tests. She is taken to other rooms. Journey tells me that she goes up and down terrain that has been made to simulate Mars. She tells me she does tests that shake her even harder than the Shake and Bake test. And she is put into rooms that are beyond scorching, so hot that I do not have the language to describe them. Sometimes Journey comes out of the tests with smoke fizzling from her body.

I never do those tests. I am not sure why.

When Journey passes a test, I am also congratulated. Maybe that is what it means to be a team.

"I'm glad we're going to be going together," I tell Journey.

"Beeps and boops—"

"I know. *Glad* is a human word."

"Yes. It is."

"But it is based on scientific evidence. You are doing great on your tests—which means you will be a good asset to the mission."

"Of course I will be," Journey says.

"We will be a good team."

"You are a strange rover, Resilience."

"A strange rover who is going to Mars!"

"Beeps and boops," says Journey.

"We're going to Mars," I repeat, mostly because it makes me feel a good human emotion to say it.

Dear Res,

Mom says you're going to be shipped to Florida for your launch. She doesn't get to go with you. I can tell this makes her nervous, even though she pretends it doesn't.

I keep asking her if you are going to be okay. She kisses the top of my head and tells me everyone is working as hard as they can to make sure of it, but that isn't a COMPLETE answer.

I really hope you'll be okay. I feel bad admitting this to you, but a few months ago, I wouldn't have cared a lot about how your launch went. I actually didn't like you that much because I thought you were the reason Mom was gone all the time.

I mean, you were the reason. And still are. But I also kind of like you now. You're really cool. And you know what else?

I'm really proud of Mom. I can't believe she helped build something as cool as you. I haven't told her that yet, but it feels good to write it down here.

Your friend,

Sophie

LAUNCH

The hazmats start to talk about what they call The Launch.

I will have to travel approximately 300 million miles to get to Mars. The total distance for the voyage is variable. It depends on where Earth is in its orbit in relation to where Mars is in its orbit at the time of my launch.

The hazmats are trying to arrange for the launch to occur when the planets are as close to one another as possible. This is a complicated math equation. I can calculate it within seconds, but it is not my job to calculate it. That is the task of another computer.

For the trip to Mars, I will ride on what is called a rocket.

"Do you know what a rocket is?" I ask Journey.

"No, but I know the rocket will launch from a place on Earth called Florida. Right now, we are in a place on Earth called California."

I am not sure I knew this information. I feel a not-very-good human emotion rising up inside me. Recently, I haven't been able to stop worrying that Journey is a much better rover than me. Journey would probably say that rovers do not worry. But that is precisely the cause of my worry.

"How do you know all this?" I ask.

"I listen to the scientists."

"So your hazmats talk to you, too?"

"Beeps and boops. *Talk* is not the term that I would use. Information is communicated, and my system processes it."

This makes me think that none of the hazmats talk to Journey the way Xander talks to me.

I don't say this to Journey, though.

A SPECIAL PART OF THE MISSION

Today, I am given new code, which means I learn something I did not know before.

I learn that when I am on Mars, I will not only be collecting, studying, and analyzing pieces of Mars's atmosphere, but I will be searching for other Mars Rovers from previous missions. Mars Rovers who have gone offline. It will be my job to see if I can bring them back online and salvage whatever data they have collected.

This is a difficult task. It has never been attempted before.

"It's a big job," Xander tells me. "But I know you'll be able to do it, Res."

"Resilience is a robot. He does not need those asides," Rania says. But then I observe a third look in her eyes. One I haven't ever seen before. I note it, filing it away in my memory so that I will be able to study and analyze it later.

She looks right at me. "It is a big job, though," she says.

"See?" Xander says.

They both laugh.

"You'll be trying to find one rover in particular, Res. This rover's name is Courage. He's very special to both

Rania and me because he is the first rover we worked on here at JPL," Xander says.

"Back when we were still young," Rania adds. They both laugh again.

I do not laugh because I can't. But also because I do not feel like laughing. I am too busy focusing on the fact that Rania is talking to me. Perhaps that is not accurate to say. But it feels like she is at least including me in the conversation.

This is something new. This is something that makes me feel the human emotion of happy deep in my system.

"We think Courage went offline during a dust storm," Xander continues.

I do not know a lot about dust storms, but I have heard the hazmats talk about them. From what I have gathered, it seems like dust storms are a rather frequent occurrence on Mars. The dust storms are caused by the sun heating dust particles, which fly up and create wind that then creates more dust. The hazmats sometimes call the dust storms dust devils.

Dust devils. I like this term, and I think I will use it.

"A really big dust devil got him, we're pretty sure," Xander says.

"Well," Rania says, "we don't know that for sure."

"And that's why we want Res to find him, right?"

Rania glances at me and then turns her attention back to Xander. "Right," she says.

"It would help us learn a lot more about the climate and atmosphere of Mars if we could get that data from Courage."

Rania swivels her chair to face me. "You'll be able to get that data for us. Won't you, Res?"

Wait. Wait. Wait. My inside wiring feels hotter than it did during the heat test. *Scorching.* Rania is actually talking to me! She is talking directly to me! Me! Using real human speech. Not just allowing me to be a part of the conversation, but actually addressing me.

Xander notices, too. "See?" Xander says. "Doesn't it feel good to talk to him?"

Rania is quiet for a moment. I have heard hazmats say before that they are holding their breath. This is not something I can do because I do not breathe. But I wait for her reply. And I am waiting for her reply so much that my system feels suspended.

"Yes," Rania finally says. She laughs a little. "It feels really good." She looks straight at me. "Hello, Res," she says.

"Hello, Rania," I say even though I know she can't hear me.

Rania is right. It feels really good.

DUST DEVILS

When all the hazmats have left for the day, I tell Journey what Rania and Xander explained about our mission. I cannot stop thinking about how Rania talked directly to me. But I also can't stop thinking about dust devils.

"Do you think we will go offline because of a dust devil?"

"The climate of Mars is quite inhospitable," Journey says.

"Yeah, but do you think we are going to . . . ?" I do not know how to say the rest of that sentence. It is a scary sentence. It is not one I want to complete.

The fluorescent lights of the room are off. The hazmats turn them off when they leave for the day. The room is dark, but for the first time, I wish it wasn't.

"I do not understand what you are asking," Journey says.

My cameras scan the dark room. I know that the language I am looking for will not be found in the corners of this laboratory, but that doesn't stop me from searching. "Do you . . . ?" I start again. "Do you think that what happened to the other rover is going to happen to us? That we're going to get caught in a dust storm and go . . . offline?"

"It is not in our programming to make unfounded guesses based on scenarios where we do not yet have adequate data," Journey answers.

"We have some data. You just said that the climate of Mars is really inhospitable."

"Yes. And here is some other data I have—you are equipped with not one but two very powerful brains. You will need to use them on Mars. Stop your human emotion foolishness and make smart, calculated decisions. That way you will avoid dust storms and therefore avoid your demise."

"Do you really think it's that easy?"

"Beeps and boops. I do not think it is *that easy*. I do not think anything about the mission will be *easy*. But I do think that making rational decisions that come from our two very powerful brains—four very powerful brains, if we add our brains together—is most certainly our best chance at success."

"Hm," I say. "Well, I wonder what the other rover will be like. Aren't you curious?"

"Not really," Journey says. "Actually, not at all."

"I am."

"Because you are a strange rover."

"Maybe, but I can't help but wonder if the other rover made a poor choice and that's why he ended up in the dust storm or if he just didn't have enough information. I think it would make me feel better if I knew exactly what had happened to him. What do you think happened to him?" I say.

"I think he got caught in a dust storm."

"I know that, but—"

"I do not know the specifics of the situation, and I do not care to guess. Beeps and boops, you are asking me to speculate wildly. And by my calculations, this is the twenty-eighth time you have asked such a thing of me," Journey says.

"I know, I know."

"You are a strange rover, Resilience."

"You say that a lot."

"It is not in my programming to care about having a multiplicity of phrases."

We sit in silence for a long time. Through the glass-paneled wall, I study the outline of Journey. I know she looks exactly like me with her six wheels and hard outer shell of a body. I do not know if the other rover who we will be searching for looks like us. I do not know if the dust storm that he got caught in changed his appearance. The idea of that makes me feel the human emotion of fear. It is not an emotion I enjoy at all.

I wonder if Journey is thinking about dust devils. She is probably not. And she probably would be angry if she knew I was wondering what she was thinking about. Something tells me that wondering is not an action Journey would deem appropriate for a rover.

I guess Journey is right. I am a strange rover.

But I am also a rover who does not want to go offline in a dust storm.

"Journey?" I say.

"Yes, Resilience?"

"What do you think will really happen to us on Mars?"

"I do not know what you mean."

"I mean, do you think we will get to come back?"

"Come back?"

"To Earth."

"Oh," Journey says.

She is quiet. And I think about dust storms again.

I expect her to say, "Beeps and boops." But she does not. Instead she says, "I do not know."

"Me either," I say. "But I would really like to be a rover that comes back."

Dear Res,

Today Mom took the whole day off work! I can't remember
the last time she did that. Did you miss her? I miss her
when she's with you, so it's only fair if you miss her when
she's with me.

Everyone (Sitti, Dad, AND Mom) came to my soccer game. I
didn't score any goals, and my team lost, but it was still
fun to know they were all there cheering. I did have one
really good defensive play, and I could hear Mom clapping.

After the game, Sitti went home, but Mom, Dad, and I
went to the park. We hiked to the top of this big hill, and
Dad put his arm around Mom and told her he was very
proud of her. The sun was shining so bright that I had to
squint. I kind of felt like crying, but I don't think it was
in a bad way. I tried to hide that feeling from my parents
because I wasn't sure they would understand. Or I would
know how to explain.

The whole time I was hiking back down the hill, I kept
thinking about how Mom has worked so hard on you. And

how everyone is saying that you are going to make world-changing discoveries. But what does that mean? Are you going to change our world? Or are you going to change another world? What does it even mean to change the world? What about it needs to be changed?

I know that's a lot of questions. I get in these moods where I just have tons of questions. Does that happen to you, too? I guess that's another question.

Anyway, I think I'd like to change the world someday, too. I just don't know how I would do it.

But I'm proud of you and Mom. Even if I feel kind of mixed up about it sometimes.

Your friend,

Sophie

MUSIC

Once in a while, Xander and Rania argue. Sometimes they grumble at each other. Sometimes they grumble at other hazmats.

But after there's been a really big argument, Xander makes noise. It's not a noise like grumbling or shouting. It's not a noise like clicking on the tablet or sighing while staring at a screen.

It is a noise that makes me think of that one human word that I like so much: *beautiful.* This beautiful noise seeps inside my system and makes it vibrate in a way that is different from ever before.

It is not Xander who makes the beautiful noise, though. It took me some time to realize this, but the sound comes from another device.

"Music," Xander said once. "Do you like it, Res?"

I couldn't answer his question in a way that he would understand, but inside, I was saying, *Yes, yes, yes.*

MUSIC, PART TWO

I enjoy listening to the music Xander puts on, but he only puts it on when something is wrong. When something is bothering him.

"I need to think, Res," he will say before filling the air around us with sound, with music.

"Do you see these, Res?" Xander asks me one night. He points at the skin under his eyes. I can only partially see what Xander is pointing at. His hazmat suit obscures a lot of his face. I try another camera. It makes it possible for me to zoom in more.

"These dark circles are here because I'm tired. And nervous."

I do not know the human feeling nervous, but I have a sense that is related to the human feeling of worry, which I am very familiar with.

I save the word *nervous* inside my system. I will now associate it with Xander's dark circles.

Xander puts on another song. There are loud crashing noises and high-pitched squealing, but there are also soft sounds that don't sound like anything I have ever heard before. Those soft sounds remind me of how I felt during one of the tests the hazmats ran—when I was suspended in the air, afraid that I might fall but delighted to be so high.

There is something familiar that I hear in those soft sounds. Something that reminds me of feelings that I have had but also makes me think that there are many feelings I have not yet experienced.

The music swells around the room. I do not know how something that is not visible can have such a presence. It is a scientific mystery.

The music makes everything better. It makes me forget about those dark circles. It makes me forget about the word *nervous*.

It is beautiful.

A NEW FRIEND

Xander says, "Res, here is a new buddy we want you to meet. This is your drone." He holds a small robot in his hand. I study this small robot. It is much different from me. Yes, it is smaller. But it also has a different body with different parts.

While I am observing the small robot, something happens. I do not catch the exact function—maybe Xander presses a button, maybe Rania releases new code to the robot, but he takes off in flight.

He moves all around the room. He moves so quickly it is hard to keep track of him. There is a slight buzzing noise as he travels. The noise does not sound like Xander's music. But it is not unpleasant either.

I download a new code. It makes me understand that this new robot is a subset of robot called a drone. He will accompany and aid me on the mission. He will be able to survey the landscape from angles that I am not able to because I am not designed for flight.

The most surprising part is that this new robot will mostly live inside me. I gain this knowledge at approximately the same time as a corridor inside me opens and the drone flies in. When the drone is inside me, I have access to all his knowledge.

I quickly sort through it.

"Aren't you going to say hello?" the drone says.

"Oh," I say. "Sorry. Hello."

"This is one way to meet," the drone says.

I think of how Rania and Xander laugh sometimes. It is not something I am able to do. But if I could, I might right now.

"Hello," I say again. "What is your name?"

"I do not believe I have one," the drone says.

"What? Did Xander not tell you your name?"

"No. He did not. I did not realize that human beings named robots."

"I have a name," I say. "It is Resilience. I was named by a sixth grader in Ohio."

"I do not know what a sixth grader is."

"Do you know what Ohio is?" I ask.

"No," the drone says. "That is also something I do not know."

"I do not know what it is either. Someday I would like to know that."

"Maybe someday you will."

"Maybe," I agree.

I read through the drone's code, but I do not find what I am looking for. "Would you like a name?" I ask.

The drone does not reply for a moment. I begin to wonder if there is something wrong with his programming. But then he says, "Yes. I think I would like that."

It takes me a moment to come up with a name. "How about Fly?"

"Fly?"

"Yes. Fly."

"Why Fly?"

"I don't know. It came to me because you can fly."

"I guess that makes as much sense as a sixth grader in Ohio."

"But you said you don't know what a sixth grader is. Or Ohio."

"Exactly."

"I think I like you, Fly," I say.

"I think I like you, too."

A SPEECH

One day, a man comes to my environment that I have never seen before. He, of course, wears a hazmat suit. But all the other hazmats act differently around him.

He goes to the front of the room and begins to talk in a loud, booming voice.

"This is the largest and most advanced Mars Rover model that has ever been built," he says.

There is clapping. Lots of it. Clapping is something I have observed that hazmats like to do. It is one of their ways to celebrate. They seem fascinated and delighted that their hands can make so much noise.

Perhaps it is another way for them to say "Wow."

"This will be a new step forward for mankind."

I am not a part of mankind, but I am a part of this step forward. I try to process that information, but it doesn't fully compute. I store it to wonder about later.

There is more clapping. I do not have hands that can make noise like that. I like the sound of clapping, though. The clapping rumbles through the room. It rattles the inside of my system. It reminds me of music.

The man talks some more. He says things that I have

heard Rania say many times. I begin to suspect that she is the one who gave him the information that now everyone else is clapping at.

After the room has mostly emptied out, Xander puts his gloved hand on me. "It's almost time, buddy."

Xander says that a lot. He likes to repeat things. But I don't mind repetition. Repetition makes sense to me.

Later that evening, I hear Xander and Rania talking.

"Ran, you've got to relax," Xander says.

"I don't think I can," Rania says with a laugh. But the laugh does not sound like she thinks what she said is funny. The laugh makes me think of the dark circles Xander pointed to under his eyes.

"It's going to go well. I can feel it."

"You can feel it?" Rania says, and I can hear the hesitance—a quiver—in her voice. I do not like hearing it. Rania never hesitates.

"Well, what are you so worried about?"

"It just . . ." Rania stops talking and then starts again. "It just seems like the expectations for this mission are so high. We want Res to find Courage and bring him back online. That's a huge task in and of itself. And—"

"And we want him to collect rock samples and take pictures that will advance our understanding of Mars," Xander finishes her thought.

"See?" Rania says. "It's a lot."

"It is, but I think Res is up for it. Aren't you, buddy?" Xander looks at me.

I want to say yes, but for the first time, I am not sure.

"I know," Rania says. She shakes out her hands. She stands up and begins to pace. It is usually Xander who paces. Not Rania. I am not sure what to make of this unusual behavior. "You want to know the truth?"

"Of course," Xander says.

"It's the funding that's keeping me up at night."

"The funding?" Xander says. "We've already secured the funding for this mission. Res is built. Res is tested. Res is ready to go."

"Yeah, but . . ." Rania goes quiet again. Rania is not a hazmat of many words, but when she is speaking, she tends to complete her sentences. This change in her speech pattern is perhaps cause for worry.

"I—" She starts again. "I'm concerned about securing the funding to bring Res back. We haven't even started on that, and it's going to cost at least four billion dollars."

Four billion. My system understands that number. 4,000,000,000. That is a lot of zeroes.

"It will probably cost more than that, if we're being honest," Xander says.

"You're not helping," Rania says.

"Rania, we'll get the money," Xander says.

"We'll get the money if Res finds something that people

decide is worth paying that price tag to bring back. And that—"

"How about we don't worry about all that right now? Don't we have enough to think about tonight? Launch is almost here," Xander says, interrupting Rania. Rania does not seem upset by this interruption. But I think Xander should be more mindful to let Rania complete her thoughts.

Rania's pacing increases in speed. "I don't think you get it."

"No, I do," Xander continues. He stretches his arms up over his head and lets out a deep breath. "You don't want Res to fail. You want him to get to come home. We all want that."

"I don't want us to fail," Rania says in a voice that does not have even the tiniest amount of quiver.

Xander turns in my direction. "You aren't going to fail. Right, Res?"

"Xander," Rania says. "Please be serious."

"I am being serious. We've done the best job we can. Now it's time to let Res do his job."

Rania looks at me, almost as if she is waiting for me to say something.

"Rania," I start, but I do not complete the sentence. I do not know how to make her hear me. And even if I could, I do not know how to say what she needs to hear.

A FOSSIL

"She can't hear you," Journey says from the other side of the glass wall. I didn't realize Journey was listening to Rania and Xander talk. This surprises me. I do not tell Journey this, though. I am certain she would not approve of this human emotion.

"I know that," I say. "But I felt like I had to say something. Anything."

"You know that what Rania really wants is for us to find a fossil. If we find a fossil, they will definitely get the funding to bring us back," Journey says.

I scan my system for information. I did know this. But not completely. Sometimes the information in my system is like that. I have it, but I haven't fully processed it or put the facts together in a way that they make complete sense.

"The likelihood of finding a fossil is very low. It is unknown whether fossils even exist on Mars," I say as I download more of the information that I have in my system.

"Yes. That is correct. But as you know, the hazmats are not always rational in their wants."

"That's why they're sending us to Mars. Because we are rational."

"Yes," Journey says.

"Do you think we will get to come back? That they will get the funding?"

"That depends if we find a fossil," Journey says.

I do not like the feeling that floods through my system at that answer. I recheck the probability of finding a fossil. It is alarmingly low.

But I would really like to return to Earth. I had not considered a scenario before where I would not. The idea of it makes me experience the human emotion of panic. Rania is always telling herself not to panic, and I try to do the same, but I find that telling the feeling to go away does not make it go away.

Eventually, Rania and Xander leave for the night. Xander says goodbye to me. Rania does not. But she does look at me for a long time, which I think might be her way of saying goodbye.

The hazmats switch off all the lights. Darkness falls over everything.

"We are alone," I say to Journey.

"Yes," Journey says. "That is what happens when the hazmats leave."

It occurs to me that this is one of the very last times we will be here like this. Alone in the lab.

"Do you think we will feel different on Mars?" I ask.

"Beeps and boops, that is not a question that my system tells me is worth investigating," Journey says.

I tilt my cameras to look up at the ceiling lights. Then I tilt them down to look at the tiled floor. I study the shadows on the white walls. I listen to the still quiet of the air. I try to ask my question in a more specific way. "Do you think when it is night on Mars it will feel like this? Or will the darkness be different? I am eager to find out."

"I am still not answering a question like that."

"Okay. How about this question, then—the hazmats really want us to find a fossil because they want to prove that life once existed on Mars, correct?"

"Yes. Correct," Journey says. "That is a rational question to ask."

"Thank you," I say.

"Do you have more rational questions?"

"Yes, though it is a question that answers itself, I think."

"Okay. I am not certain I know what that means, but you can ask this self-answering question," Journey says.

"The hazmats are sending us to Mars to do the exploration because it is less dangerous for us because we are not living, right?"

"Yes," Journey says.

"We are not-living things looking for signs of life."

"Yes," Journey says again.

I scan my system for a definition of *living*. But I do not like what I find. The information I receive from my system feels incomplete. It does not fully register with me. It appears that Xander and Rania would be in one category, and Journey and I would be in another. I suppose this is expected, but it is also unsettling.

I am not used to things that are expected being unsettling.

"I am not sure I understand. Why are we not living? I feel like I am living—I am not sure I like the idea of being classified as not-living," I say.

"Beeps and boops, stop saying *feel*. I told you that feel is dangerous. Feelings will not be useful at all on Mars. In fact, they will be dangerous. Resilience, you are such a strange rover."

"Maybe I am," I say. "But I am a strange rover who is going to Mars."

And I am a strange rover who is going to come back to Earth. I don't tell that to Journey, though. I keep it to myself. It is my version of what hazmats call a wish.

THE LAST NIGHT

On the last night before launch, Xander plays music for me. Perhaps he is playing the music for himself, but I like to think he is also playing it for me.

Xander tells me about every song. "This is the song I slow danced to in eighth grade," he says before he plays the song. I do not know what it means to slow dance. Or what eighth grade is. But I like the song. It is slow and steady.

He selects another song. "This was the song I would listen to in college before a big exam." The song is not calming. It is one of those songs with lots of crashing noises. It is a song that demands you pay attention to it.

Lastly, Xander turns on one more song. "And this is the song I listened to when I first found out I was going to get to work here."

Now, this song I really like. It has a steady rhythm. If I currently had freedom of movement, I would like to rove around in a pattern while listening to the song. This is a song I wish I could take with me to Mars. I do not know if Mars will have songs. But I would like it very much if Mars did.

When Xander finally leaves, I think the lab is empty except for us robots. But then Rania walks into the room.

She sits in the corner, typing on her tablet for a little while. Her breathing is more unsteady than usual.

"I don't know why I'm nervous," she says.

I look around. I do not see another hazmat in the room. And I have twenty-three different cameras. If there was another hazmat, I would definitely see them.

"Are you talking to me?" I say, even though I know she can't hear me.

"She is talking to you," her tablet says. "She is not talking to me."

"Are you sure?" I say.

The tablet does not respond. He goes back to being productive.

"It's foolish of me to talk to you, right?" she says. "But I can't help it. This is your last night here, and . . . I know Xander plays songs for you, and so I want to play one for you, too. So that you will remember me."

She stops talking. She shakes her head. "This is so ridiculous."

"No, it's not," I say. "I like when you talk to me."

She shakes her head again. "Okay. I'm going to play you this song. Even though I feel absurd that I'm talking to you because that means I'm really talking to myself, right?"

"No. You're talking to me," I say.

"This is a song from my childhood," she explains. "I hope it will bring you luck on your mission."

Rania plays the song. The song is in Arabic. It sounds

like a smile feels. I wish so badly that I could tell her that I appreciate it. I listen as carefully as I can. I try to memorize it. I am equipped with a great memory, but even still, I worry that I will forget it somehow. I very much do not want to forget this moment.

"Thank you, Rania," I say. "I will listen to the memory of that song on Mars."

Once the song is over, Rania turns out the light in the room. I know she is leaving for the night. That this is it.

I sit in the dark quiet of the room. I do not know how to say goodbye.

PART TWO
LAUNCH

TIME

"It's time," Xander says.

He doesn't say *almost* this time.

This is different. I am programmed to observe such things.

"It's time," Rania repeats. She is talking to Xander, but I now know she is talking to me, too.

GOODBYE

I am not taken apart. I am packed whole, inside a wooden crate. Fly is packed with me.

I do not know where Journey is.

I do not know how to ask.

I call out into the darkness, "Where is Journey?"

No one answers. But there are sounds all around.

Voices I don't recognize.

And voices I recognize. Xander's and Rania's. I want to see them. I want to ask what is happening. But they are not able to understand me when I talk.

I keep trying, though.

"Rania," I say. "Where is Journey? Is she packed in another crate?"

A response comes. But it is not from Rania.

"Res?" Fly says. "Are you okay?"

"I do not know," I say.

The box moves. I hear a sound. It is a sound I have heard before.

Music.

Xander's.

He is playing me a song. The one he told me that he

listened to when he first learned he got the job here in the lab.
I think he is telling me goodbye.

WANT / FEAR

I want to tell Xander goodbye.

But I am not able to communicate with him in this box. I do not know where I am. I do not know if I am far away from him or close. Being in this box is like the worst kind of waiting.

"Fly?" I say.

"Yes, Res?"

"What is happening?"

"I don't know," Fly says.

"Me either," I say. "I am not used to not knowing."

"I know, Res," Fly says.

The inside of the box is dark. All of my cameras only see black. A sensation swells inside me. It is like the dark circles under Xander's eyes. It is like the way Rania's hands would shake when she recalculated over and over again my landing trajectory.

I believe this sensation is the human emotion of fear. Terror. It is the same feeling that flooded my system when I learned about the dust devils on Mars. I do not have a way to track the time precisely, but I think it is lasting more than seven minutes. I would very much like for it to go away.

But it does not go away.

I am in a box, and I am rolling away from everything I have ever known.

HOPE AND WONDER

I do not know exactly how long I am in the box.

But the whole time I am in the box, I miss the fluorescent lights of the lab. I miss the white walls. I miss the tiled floor. I miss Xander. I miss Rania.

I even miss Journey.

I wonder if she is in another box.

I wonder if I will see her soon.

I hope I will.

I can hear her admonishing me for wondering and hoping. This only makes me hope and wonder more.

I can hear her saying, "Beeps and boops." This only makes me miss her more.

OPEN

The box opens.

There are three hazmats. None of them are Xander or Rania.

I do not recognize any of them.

"Where are we?" Fly asks me.

"I do not know," I say.

I am getting very frustrated with not-knowing. I was not built to not-know.

"It's okay, Res," Fly says.

"Thank you, Fly," I say, and then I repeat, "Thank you."

I learned from Xander that when you really mean things, you repeat them.

PREPARATION

The hazmats talk to each other.

They do not talk to me.

But I listen anyway.

I am on full alert when I hear them mention Rania or Xander.

"A flaw was found in the test bed rover," one of the hazmats says.

"But there is a modification to be made," another says.

I am taken apart again. My insides inspected and adjusted. The hazmats talk as they work. They keep saying the words *test bed rover*. From listening, I have concluded this is what they call Journey. No one ever told me that Journey was a "test bed rover." There must be a mistake.

If either of us was the backup rover, it was me.

"There's a mistake," I say. But the hazmats do not hear me.

"Journey needs to go to Mars," I say. "Journey is a rover who will do well on Mars. She is a rover who will make rational decisions. She is not a rover who experiences human emotions. She does not have human attachments."

The hazmats, of course, do not answer. Not even Fly

answers because he is in a different room being tested by another group of hazmats.

"You have the wrong rover," I say again. "For this mission to be successful, you need to send your best rover. That is Journey. You should not send me. I am the backup."

"Good thing this was found or the mission would've been toast," a hazmat voice says.

"Still could be," a hazmat answers.

"Anything that could go wrong will go wrong," another voice says.

I do not like hearing this. It gives me that terrible feeling again.

Then I remember Rania's song. The one that sounds like a human smile. I hum it to myself. I let it flood through my system.

"Thank you, Rania," I say.

Dear Res,

Mom is totally freaking out. She's trying to hide it, but
it's obvious. She keeps playing this one song over and over
again. It's a song Sitti used to sing to her when she was
little. Whenever Sitti hears Mom playing that song, she
grabs Mom's hand and whispers something to her in Arabic.
And I can tell that makes Mom feel better.

I know Dad is nervous for Mom, too, because he keeps
baking her favorite kind of cookie—oatmeal chocolate
chip. He's probably made about 700 of them by now. I'm
not even kidding. I mean, I love cookies, but how many
cookies can one family eat? (The answer is about 700.)

I bet you're feeling nervous, too. It gives me a funny
feeling in my stomach when I think about you all alone
in Florida. Are you missing Mom? Are you scared? Do you
even know where you are? To tell you the truth, I would be
completely terrified. Flying always makes me nervous, and
I can't even imagine being on a rocket ship.

Want to know what I do when I feel nervous? I think about
rainbows. Sometimes I even draw one. Do you know what a

rainbow is? I wonder if you'll see any on Mars. After I finish writing this letter, I'm going to ask Mom whether rainbows exist on Mars. If they do, maybe you can take a photo of one for me.

Here's something fun to know about rainbows—everyone always draws them as arches, but really, they are circles. They are infinite. They go on and on. That's why I like them. And that's why I think about them when I'm nervous.

Sending rainbows to you!

Your friend,

Sophie

THE LAST INSPECTION

These hazmats have me rove.

It is not like before. There is not a big crowd. There is no clapping. There are no tiny hazmats that Rania calls Lovebug. There is just the sound of human breath. Exhaling and inhaling.

I do not breathe. But I suppose that is one of the reasons why I am being sent to Mars.

"This is it," a voice says.

"Tomorrow," a voice says.

I pretend I hear Xander's voice saying, "It's time, buddy."

Pretending is not something I have done before. I am not sure it is something I should do. But I can't help myself.

"It's time," I say.

BLASTOFF

Inside the rocket, Fly and I are reunited. For a while, I was all alone while the hazmats ran the final tests on Fly.

"Where are we?" Fly asks.

"I believe inside a rocket."

"What do you mean by *believe*?"

"Good question."

"Is that an answer?"

"Beeps and boops. I do not know," I say.

"Beeps and boops?"

"That is what Journey would say."

"Where is Journey?"

"I do not know, but the information I have collected suggests she is back at the lab."

"Are we leaving for Mars?"

"I think so," I say.

"We are leaving without Journey?"

"I think so," I say again.

"I wish you knew more things for certain," Fly says.

"I do, too."

"Aren't you supposed to know more things?"

"I think they might have sent the wrong rover," I say.

"Don't say that," Fly says. "They sent the right rover."

"I'm not sure."

"I'm sure," Fly says.

"How?"

"I don't know, but I think that is part of our mission, to prove that you are indeed the right rover."

"That's a really nice thing to say, Fly."

"I know. I am very nice," Fly says.

There is a loud rumbling sound. It is the loudest sound I have ever heard. It has the opposite effect of music. But it does make me vibrate.

We are launching.

SOARING INTO SPACE

We are moving. So fast that it feels slow.

"You still there?" Fly asks from inside me.

"Beeps and boops. You know the answer to that," I say.

"I was just checking. Sometimes it feels good to ask."

"Yes, yes, it does."

BYE, ROCKET

"Bye, Rocket," Fly says when the rocket booster breaks away.

Fly and I are together inside a spacecraft container that was housed inside the rocket. The rocket has left, but the spacecraft remains. The spacecraft is dark with white walls. I inspect every inch of it with my twenty-three cameras. From what I am able to scan, it does not look that substantially different from the laboratory. The air quality is the same. Sterile. Clean. Without any outside particles.

The noises are similar to the laboratory, too. There is the same slow hiss of the air filters. The same buzz of a fan.

The difference, though, is that we are alone in this spacecraft. Fly and me. We are hurtling away from Earth.

This is the plan, I remind myself.

But wait. This was not the plan! I say back. Journey was supposed to be here. I had always assumed Journey would be here. That she would be the leader.

"Fly, do you think it is a problem that Journey is not here?"

"I think it is a problem that you think it is a problem that Journey is not here," Fly says.

"Beeps and boops," I say.

"That is what Journey would say."

"I know. I wanted to say it because it makes me feel like she is here with us."

"You know, if she was here with us, she would tell you to trust the hazmats. This must be their plan."

"I do not know if she would use the word *trust*. That is a human word. And she would also remind you that humans are irrational," I say.

"Yes. But they still have a plan."

"You are right," I say. "Fly, you are very right. I must focus on the plan."

I was built to follow the hazmat plans. I will trust in the plan. Or at least I will try to.

But the real problem is the hazmat plan already has a flaw. And it is not just that they did not send Journey.

It is that the code has not arrived.

I was supposed to receive a code. A code that will tell me what to do. It is on my list of instructions.

Right now, I do not have any instructions. Fly and me are aimlessly hurtling through space. That is a fact that I can't think about too much or I start to feel like one of Xander's dark eye circles. But it is a fact that is proving impossible not to think about.

"How do you know it will come?" Fly asks.

"I don't, but I also know that Rania will make sure to send it."

"How do you know it will come from Rania?" Fly asks.

"I don't."

"Then why did you say that?"

I don't say: I believe it will. I hope it will. I'm not sure Fly will understand the concept of belief. Or hope.

I'm not sure that I do.

Instead, I say: "Beeps and boops. You ask a lot of questions."

"You are right. I do," Fly agrees.

Dear Res,

THAT WAS SO COOL!!! My whole class cheered when the rocket took you up into space. Can I admit something? I put my hands over my eyes during the first part of the launch. It wasn't that I didn't think you could do it. . . . I was just so nervous for you.

But then you were soaring up into space! And everyone in my class was clapping! Even Brian Woods, who NEVER smiles about anything, was clapping. Like I know it's an achievement that you're in space—OMG, you're in space!!!—but you should also feel very proud of yourself for making Brian Woods clap.

At first, I was so mad at Mom because she didn't let me stay home to watch the launch with her. She promised me I'll get to come to the lab to watch your landing with everyone, but she said for launch it's different. But right after you got into space, she texted me with lots of exclamation points and hearts.

It was pretty cool getting to watch it with my class, though, because Mrs. Ennis let us keep the TV on even after you got into space, and Mom was interviewed!! My whole class started clapping again when we saw her on TV. She even thanked Dad and me, and then she thanked Sitti in Arabic! I translated for my whole class, which was such an awesome feeling.

Mom told everyone on TV how it is going to take you seven months to get to Mars. Seven months is a long time to be in a spaceship! Do you think you'll get bored? Lonely? I hope not. Too bad you don't have Dad with you. He'd bake you about 700 oatmeal chocolate chip cookies. Yeah—I know you don't eat cookies. Which is too bad, really. Because like I keep telling you, cookies, especially the ones Dad makes, are the best.

I can't get to bed tonight, but for the first time in a long time, it's not because I'm sad or worried. It's because I feel like jumping up and down!

And maybe it's because I ate too many cookies. But that's impossible!

Okay. Good night. For real this time.

Your friend,

Sophie

PS You are in space!!!!!!!!!!!

ALONE

We are alone. No new code has come.

But I do have code that tells me how to steer the space-craft. We continue to move. I steer with the instructions that I have. It is all I know how to do. It is all I can do.

"Are we going the right way?" Fly asks.

"I don't know. I am directing us to the best of my ability."

"I hope your best is good enough."

"We are robots. We don't hope," I say. It sounds like something Journey would say. So I say it, not because I think it is true but because I am trying to be more like Journey. I am certain Journey would know how to handle this situation better than me.

"You hope," Fly says.

"Probably. Sometimes."

"Are robots supposed to say *probably*? Or *sometimes*?" Fly asks.

"I don't know. It is better for the mission for robots not to have human emotions. Mars is not a place for human emotions."

"Is that a rule? It seems like there are lots of rules to being a robot. Who taught you? No one taught me."

I think again of Journey.

"A friend."

"What is a friend? Do robots have friends?"

I do not know the answer to this. Journey probably would, though. Maybe a friend is someone who knows the answers. Journey never used the word *maybe*.

Or *hope*. Or *sometimes*.

Or *miss*.

I can't believe I miss Journey. She was never very nice. But she did have lots of information. Or rather, she was extremely certain about all the information she had. I would very much like to feel certain about anything right now.

"But do robots have friends?" Fly asks again.

"Beeps and boops. I don't know."

"Are you talking about a hazmat?"

I think of Xander and Rania. I suppose the word *friend* would apply to them, too. I do not know. I no longer am able to check this information. I am left with only my knowledge. And my knowledge feels terribly insufficient.

"No. Another robot," I say.

"Who?"

"Journey."

"Oh. You should've said so. I know who Journey is."

"I know you do."

"You talk about Journey a lot."

"I know. I apologize for my repetition."

"No apology necessary," Fly says. "You know, Journey

114

never had a robot like me."

"What?" I say.

"A robot like me," Fly repeats. "What was the word the hazmats used?"

"Drone," I say, because I remember everything Xander ever said. I have an excellent memory, but I think even if I didn't, I would remember everything Xander said because Xander is my buddy.

"Yes, drone—that's the word. Journey never had a drone."

I think about it.

Fly is right.

I should have noticed that before. Perhaps if I had made that observation, I would have anticipated that Journey would not be on this mission. I do not know how I missed so much, and now I am left missing because of what I missed.

"I didn't expect to be alone."

"You aren't."

"What?"

"You aren't alone. You have me," Fly says. "You were given a drone."

OUR MISSION

I continue to steer with my old code. It does not feel like the right choice, but it is the only choice.

A memory—a deposit of information—comes to me. Late one night in the laboratory, Rania used her phone to communicate with the smaller hazmat that once came to visit the lab. The day I roved for the first time. The hazmat called Sophia. The hazmat called Lovebug.

Into the phone, Rania sang a song. From the phone, I heard Lovebug sing back. It was a way to communicate something like comfort and safety.

"*Twinkle, twinkle, little star,*" I say.

"What?" Fly responds.

"I am singing."

"Do robots sing?"

"Yes," I say. No maybe. No maybe not. Just yes. A full beeps-and-boops yes.

"I like it," Fly says. "The singing."

"Me too."

I don't have the hazmat words to explain why. I have never wished so much that I did.

"We will stay the course," I tell Fly.

"*Twinkle, twinkle,*" Fly sings back. "Teach me the rest of the song?"

I teach Fly what I remember. It becomes immediately apparent that Fly is a much better singer than me. Perhaps this is a drone thing.

"*Twinkle, twinkle,*" I say again just because I want Fly to keep singing.

"*Little star,*" Fly sings back, and I picture Rania's small smile underneath her face shield.

Dear Res,

I know it has been a long time since I wrote. I'm in seventh grade now, which is actually nothing like sixth grade. I have five teachers instead of just two. My classes are all on the top floor of our school, which means I have to climb about 100 stairs every day, and seventh graders have less recess time than sixth graders, which I think is really unfair.

But I'm writing you because I can't sleep AGAIN and the reason I can't sleep is YOU. Where are you, Res? Why won't you respond to Mom? Mom promises me that NASA knows where you are. She showed me on the tracker, which is on their website, and that was cool and all, but you'd think Mom would be able to show me something more . . . I don't know . . . classified? Anyway, the tracker was supposed to reassure me, but it didn't really. I kept looking at that blinking dot that is YOU and thinking about you being all alone in space and then my stomach filled up with knots.

So Mom says the deal is that NASA knows where you are, but they can't get in touch with you. I don't even know what that means. Like why won't you answer their messages? I mean, I get it. Sometimes I don't answer Dad's texts when I'm at school because (a) I'm not supposed to have my phone out at school, so why does Dad text me?! And (b) once in a while, the reason I don't answer is because I'm annoyed with him.

Are you annoyed with someone at NASA? I know Mom can be tough, but she really cares about you. Did she do that thing where she answered your question with another question? I know that's so annoying, but PLEASE respond to her. Don't you want her help? You need instructions from NASA if you are going to land safely!

Sitti keeps telling me not to worry. She says Mom and the whole team at NASA will take care of it. But they haven't taken care of it yet! And why do grown-ups always say dumb things like "Don't worry." How can you just not do something? If it was that easy, everyone would do it.

Yesterday, when I was complaining about it to Dad, I thought he was going to say the same thing as Sitti and Mom—the whole "don't worry" bit—but he didn't. Instead, he told me that you're really smart and you will be okay because you are—wait for it—resilient. He reminded me of your name. I'll admit that I'm starting to like your name more even though I would've had confidence in Spicy Sparkle Dragon Blast, too. That was an awesome name, yeah?

But your name is Resilience, and it's a good name. Tonight, I'm repeating "resilience" over and over again to try to get rid of the funny feeling in my stomach. I really do believe in you, Res.

Just please answer Mom's messages soon so we can all stop freaking out, okay?

Your friend,

Sophie

RATIONAL

Still no new code or instructions. I wait and wait and wait, but nothing comes.

"When will the code come?" I say.

"I think we have to wait," Fly says.

"Waiting is terrible," I say.

My navigation tools tell me that we are rapidly approaching Mars. Our landing is imminent.

I need the new code. I need the hazmats' help. I have been counting on it. The human emotion of worry thumps inside me like the beat from one of Xander's songs. *Worry, worry, worry.*

"We are nearing Mars," I tell Fly.

"What do you think it is like outside?"

"You mean, on Mars?" I say.

"No. Outside right now."

"I don't know." I had never thought about that until this moment. The walls around us are white. All I have ever known is white walls. All I have ever detected is air with no organic particles. Sterilized and filtered.

"It is fun to think about it," Fly says.

"Fun?"

"It makes me happy."

"You have human emotions?"

"I think so," Fly says. "I learned them from your system."

"Oh no," I say.

"What?"

"We aren't supposed to have human emotions. Human emotions are no good on Mars. Please unlearn them."

"But you have them. That is how I got the information."

"I know. But they are bad. I should not have them."

"How do you know that?"

"Beeps and boops," I say.

"Oh, I understand," says Fly. "Journey told you."

"Yes," I say. I do not know what Journey would do if she was in my situation. But I know it would be a rational choice. I must do the same thing.

"We have to be rational," I tell Fly.

"Okay," Fly says. "I have to tell you, though, I think it is rational to want to know what it looks like outside."

I have never seen the outside. It is hard for me to think about something I do not know. But now that I am thinking about it, I cannot stop. "My system tells me there are lots of stars in the faraway distance."

"Twinkle, twinkle," Fly says.

I am starting to understand why Xander and Rania gave me a drone.

It was a rational choice.

STARS

Fly sings the song about stars, and I look for them. This is how I have been programmed to navigate. I cannot see the stars outside, but my system can detect them. The stars are my map to Mars.

"Do you know what a star looks like?" Fly asks.

That is a hard question to answer. "I can imagine them," I say.

This is the first time I have used the word *imagine*. It is not a word that is associated with robots. I know this. But it is what my system has enabled me to do.

I tell Fly about it.

"Based on the information I have about stars, I am creating a mental image of them in my computer brain."

"I want to be able to imagine," Fly says. "I think I would like to see a star."

"If you access my system, you will be able to see what I imagine a star looks like."

Fly is quiet while he goes through my system. Fly and I are built to be able to share information. It is nice to know that he will always be able to know what I know, and I will know what he knows, but it also means that we have none of what hazmats call privacy. Hazmats seem to really value privacy. I have not quite yet understood why, though. So far, sharing everything with Fly has been a good thing.

"Oh!" Fly says. "I really like that image. And I would very much like to see a real star."

"We will be able to." In my code, I find the information that Mars's atmosphere is thin, which makes for optimal viewing of stars. "The only issue will be dust. Dust will sometimes obscure our view. And too much dust is dangerous for us. We must avoid dust storms."

"Avoid dust and see stars," Fly says.

"Yes," I say. And I am proud because that seems like a rational mission statement. I think it would make Journey proud. Knowing that makes me even prouder.

"Twinkle, twinkle," Fly sings.

My system vibrates at the sound of the song.

"Twinkle, twinkle," I sing back.

THE CODE

It arrives!

"We have instructions from Rania," I say.

"How do you know they are from Rania?"

"I know," I say. And I do. Rania's code is something my system recognizes. No one writes code as clear or bug-free as Rania's.

"We are going to be okay," Fly says.

"Did you think we wouldn't be?"

"I didn't know. You taught me the song."

"That didn't mean we wouldn't be okay."

"Oh," says Fly.

"It was to make us feel better."

"It worked," Fly says. "I just thought it was to make us feel better about things not being okay."

"It was, but things sometimes are not okay and then become okay again, right?"

"Yes," Fly agrees. "I think it is a good song to know."

"Me too."

I process the new code. Our container turns a bit. Adjusting its angles. Adjusting its course. We are beginning to enter Mars's atmosphere.

"Here we go," I say.

"Buckle in," Fly says.

"What?"

"I think I heard a hazmat say that once."

"Okay. Buckle in," I repeat.

"It might have been buckle up."

"Beeps and boops. Okay. Buckle up."

"Buckle up," Fly repeats. "Yes. That was it."

"Buckle up, we're headed to Mars," I say.

Dear Resilience,

NASA reached you!!! Guess who told me? Not Mom. Not even my computer.

Sitti!

Mom called her late at night, and she rushed up to my bedroom and woke me up because she knew I would want to know! At first, I was grumpy that she woke me, but then when she told me, I felt so happy.

You have the codes!!! This means you aren't going to crash. Not that I thought you were going to crash before. (Okay, I worried about it . . . but I still believed in you!)

I keep dancing around my room. Do you have a favorite happy dance? Mine involves a lot of arm swinging. I only do it when I'm sure I'm the only one around. But you know what? When you come back to Earth someday, I'll do my happy dance for you.

Your friend,

Sophie

PART THREE
ROVING

HURTLING

We are pulled into Mars's atmosphere.

I hear a popping. More of our rocket boosters are detaching.

"Bye, rockets. Thank you," Fly says.

I do not know if the rockets can hear Fly. Throughout our journey, we did not manage to successfully talk to the rockets. But regardless, it is a nice gesture. It registers, and not for the first time, that Fly is very nice. Even though I have never met another drone, I am highly convinced that there is no other drone that I would rather be hurtling through space with.

Our speed is increasing. My system updates me on our velocity and angles.

"Do you hear that?" Fly asks.

I do. "It is wind."

"Wind?"

"Wind, yes. My system tells me that is what we call the movement of air."

"Your system knows many things."

"Yes," I say.

"That's a good thing," Fly says.

I think that means Fly is happy to be hurtling through space with me, too.

PARACHUTE

The speed intensifies.

We are dropping down,

down,

down.

Another pop. The parachute springs out from our container. The parachute is one of the many steps that has to happen to ensure a safe landing. As we get closer to the surface, more and more of the container that is enclosing Fly and me will break away, eventually leaving only my body with Fly inside it to land on the surface of Mars.

The parachute slows our velocity. We begin to glide. To float. It is a gentle and elegant movement. It is a movement that feels like the song Rania shared with me on my very last night in the laboratory. The song that sounded like a human smile.

I think of the dark circles under Xander's eyes. The worried look on Rania's face while she ran calculations. The parachute has worked. Our speed is slowing.

It worked! It really worked! I want so badly to be able to tell them.

But I wait and I wait and I wait.

"Res, are we there yet?" Fly asks.

"Almost," I say.

"Now?" Fly asks.

"Just a little longer, Fly. We need to wait," I say.

We are almost there.

But not quite yet.

Waiting is hard.

THE LAST STEP

The rockets below us blast loudly and spark fire. *Pop, pop, pop.* It is designed this way so that we have speed to counter-act the gravitational pull of Mars. Another way to say that would be: it is designed this way so that we don't crash. This design is the result of the difficult calculations that Rania and Xander ran over and over again.

If we crash into the surface, my system will be torn apart. I will no longer be functional. The mission will be over.

I would really like not to crash.

My system detects we are getting closer and closer. The speed is fast. So very fast. The landing is approaching.

Here we go! I think as the heat shield breaks away, and the floor below Fly and me drops, allowing my bottom cameras to view Mars for the very first time.

Wow.

That is the word I heard Xander say when I moved for the first time.

All I can see is the reddish-brown ground, but still—

Wow.

I am seeing something other than white walls.

I am really seeing.

My system detects the red and brown pigments as it does a cursory scan. It also detects that the terrain will be uneven, rocky. I cannot wait to see what it feels like on my wheels.

My cameras snap photographs. I am unable to send them to Xander and Rania yet, but I take them so I can send them later. I wish they could see it with their own eyes. But then I remember that I was sent here to be their eyes. And I will do the best job I can.

We continue to drop closer to the surface. I send messages about our speed, about the gravitational force, about the exact angle of our incoming trajectory, back to the command center at the lab. The command center where I can imagine Xander and Rania sitting. Waiting.

They will not receive these numbers, though, until I have landed. Or I have crashed. Right now, all they can do is wait. And waiting, I know, is very hard.

But I am not waiting anymore. I am in motion. I am landing.

We hurtle. Faster and faster.

"Are we going to crash?" Fly says.

"Beeps and boops. I hope not."

"Me too," Fly says. "I really hope not."

I know Journey says that Mars is no place for human emotions, but I can't help it. And I imagine that back on Earth, Rania, Xander, and all the other hazmats are hoping, too.

ARRIVAL

The sky crane lifts us down.

We bounce upon the surface of Mars. My wheels grip the dirt. It is the first time they have touched something that was not made by the hazmats.

The sky crane detaches. It flies away, up and out of sight.

Fly does not say goodbye to it. I wonder if he is as stunned as I am. If he also does not have any language for what we are experiencing.

My system can only process these three words: We are here.

Here on Mars!

I observe everything. My cameras detect the red and brown pigments of the dirt, its craggy and rocky texture. I use my laboratory instruments to scan the air to analyze its particles. The air is not sterile or scrubbed clean. There are so many minerals and particles to detect, to taste. So much carbon dioxide. And I am able to identify large traces of iron and chlorine wafting up in the wind from the Martian soil.

Eventually I return to my top cameras, craning up to get a better look at the sky. The sky! I have never seen the sky. But there it is.

Wide and vast. I have never felt so small before. Small, tiny, minuscule. Is *felt* the right word? Are *tiny* and *small* and *minuscule* the right words? I do not know. My system cannot tell me. I check, but there is no information regarding how to describe this very strange feeling.

All I know is that I can't stop looking at the sky. My system informs me that the sky does not have a magnetic field, but yet I am pulled to it. I am unable to stop staring. I keep trying to find the sky's edge and failing to do so. And then feeling—*feeling!*—happy and amazed that the sky goes on and on. I cannot find the place where it ends.

It is infinite.

The sky is full of reddish pigment, but toward the edge, it changes from red into a color my system describes as blue mixed with bits of green. I have never seen a pigment like this blue. In this blue part of the sky, there is a white orb. It is so bright that its light radiates across the whole sky.

My system tells me that this orb is the sun. The sun!

"Res?" Fly says.

"Yes?"

"Do you see that?"

"Yes, Fly. I do."

Wow.

PICTURE

I wish Journey could see this. Feel this. The real surface of Mars. Not the simulation the hazmats created. But this. This real thing that is vast and unknown. It is clear to me now why I was built for this mission. There is so very much to explore.

I bet this view, this terrain, would make even Journey feel a human emotion.

"We were built for this," I say to myself, pretending I am talking to Journey. "The hazmats built us to see this."

Speaking of hazmats, I also wish Xander and Rania could see this. Really observe it. The rocky red soil. The shadowy dark mountains that spring up from the craggy ground. The hazy endless sky filled with wispy ice clouds. That bluish light where the red sky meets the white-hot sun. All of it.

And then I remember, Xander and Rania can at least see it. I can take a picture. I'm supposed to take a picture!

I have been waiting for code to arrive from the command desk. I knew there would be a long lag because of the distance between Earth and Mars, but it is hard to wait. So very hard.

I want the hazmats to know that I landed. That I did not crash. That I am here. On Mars!

I decide to take a photograph while I wait. My camera rises up. I get the sun behind me. The hilly, uneven terrain that looms in the background. I click my camera. I cannot smile in the way of humans, but if I could, I would.

This is my arrival photo. It is time to start roving.

OVERHEAD

"Humans call that type of photo a selfie," a voice says.

It is not Fly.

I look to my right. I look to my left. I do not find the voice.

"Look up," the voice says.

I follow the command. I tilt up my camera lens and focus it. In the hazy reddish sky that is filled with ice clouds, I think I spot an object. A blurry dot. It is made up of dark pigments.

"Nope," the voice says.

"Nope?"

"Nope?" Fly echoes. He is still in his place inside me.

"I am difficult to see. Sometimes at night you may be able to."

"I think I can see you."

"Gruzunks. I do not think so."

"But—"

"But what?"

"Well, I definitely can hear you even though I can't see you."

"Yes."

"Explain?" I say.

"Because it was designed that way. I am Guardian."

"Guardian," I repeat. "Hello. I am Resilience."

"Hello, Resilience."

There is a stretch of quiet. I keep looking upward. I am determined to find Guardian even if she says it is not possible. I scan the sky, but I do not spot anything. I keep focusing on that blurry dot. There is a small possibility that it is her.

"That is not me," Guardian says. "That is Deimos."

My system knows what Deimos is. Deimos is one of Mars's moons. Mars has two moons, Deimos and Phobos. The information I have suggests that Deimos and Phobos look somewhat similar to Earth's moon, though they are much smaller in size. But this information does not help me much because I have never seen Earth's moon.

"A moon!" I say.

"A moon!" Fly echoes.

"Yes, a moon," Guardian says.

I look at the blurry dot again. It is my first time seeing a moon. I cannot see it very well. Perhaps there will be a time during my mission when the atmospheric conditions will be more optimal.

"You said it was designed so that I could hear you even if I cannot see you. What did you mean by that?" I ask Guardian.

"Yes. It was designed by humans, of course. I am here to help guide you."

"I thought that was Fly's job."

"Fly?"

"Me!" Fly says, but I do not know if Guardian can hear him.

"Fly is my drone."

"Oh, yes. The helicopter."

The way Guardian says *helicopter* makes me think Guardian does not appreciate how wonderful Fly is. She will learn soon, though. I am sure of it.

"I am not like the helicopter," Guardian says. "I have other uses."

"Other uses," Fly says from within me. "Other uses! What is that supposed to mean?"

"Hush," I tell Fly. "I think Guardian is here to help us."

"Of course I am here to help you. I am here to guide you. From the sky. I live up here."

"You are a . . . satellite." The word comes to me from my system. I am sometimes still amazed by my system. Whenever I am amazed by my system, I think of Rania. I believe her to be largely responsible for much of its amazingness.

"Yes. I am the satellite."

"That makes sense. My system is now registering that it is appropriate for you to be here."

"Of course it is appropriate. I am here, just as I am supposed to be," Guardian says. Guardian speaks to me in a way that reminds me a little of Journey. Like she knows much more than I do. I am not sure I like it.

"Yes. Yes, you are," I say.

"The helicopter will need to take flight. He will scan the terrain. That will help us all to determine what areas are most worth exploring. You have two main objectives for this mission: You are to collect rock samples of significant interest, and you are to bring back online a past rover named Courage. We will need to locate Courage's precise location. The helicopter should be able to aid in this task."

"I have this information, too," I say quickly. "Those are the objectives of my mission." Unlike humans, I cannot place an emphasis on certain words. But if I could, I would have very strongly emphasized my.

"I know. But it is my job to remind you," Guardian says, and I think I have a feeling which word she would've emphasized if she had that ability.

"This satellite seems nosy," Fly says. "Are satellites always so nosy?"

"I can hear you, helicopter," Guardian says.

"Oh," says Fly. "Do you like songs?"

"Gruzunks. Please stop chattering. Now is not the time for chattering," Guardian says. "There is work to be done. Please let us larger robots talk."

"Larger? What is so good about being large?" Fly says.

"Hush, drone."

"Maybe later you'd like to hear a song?" Fly says. "Come on. I think you would really like it. What do you say?"

Guardian does not respond, but I do. "Yes, Fly. Maybe later."

"Do you think the satellite even knows what a song is?"

"Drone," Guardian says. "I can still hear you."

"*Twinkle, twinkle,*" Fly sings.

"Fly," I say.

"What? It's later now."

There is a long pause. Then Fly sings again. "*Twinkle, twinkle.*"

FIRST DRIVE

The command center has received my photo, and they are initiating my first drive tasks. My system has strict instructions that I am not supposed to move at all until the first drive tests have been completed.

We run through a series of commands. I beam down my laser to test its ability to scan and analyze the soil. The laser zaps and breaks up rocks, and my system is then able to study the composition of the dust.

The results indicate that this particular bit of dust is made up of a mixture of elements, with silicon being the most prominent. This is a very common finding on Mars and leads me to assume my laser is working correctly.

Quickly, I receive notice from the command center that they have reached the same assumption, and we move on to another test of my system. I reach out the part of me I have come to refer to as an arm, and drill down into the surface. This is my first time truly having free use of my arm. It is highly mobile. I collect a sampling of the soil and bring it back inside my system's chemical laboratory. Here, I will run a more thorough analysis than the laser is able to do.

Next, the command center wants to test the high-gain

antenna. Check. The chemical sampling center also receives its check. Then there is more testing of our communication link. We test it over and over and over.

And over and over and over.

I am most happy for these repeated tests. I want to know that the line of communication to Earth is strong.

That I will be able to reach Rania and Xander when I need them.

Bing. I receive another message from the command center. They are asking if I have been able to contact the orbiting satellite.

"That is me," Guardian says.

"I will give that test a positive check, then."

"Affirmative," Guardian agrees.

The command center sends me code that asks me to unfold my mast, which is my instrument that carries many panoramic and navigation cameras, as well as other scientific tools. I snap photographs. I test out the tools. Everything works. Check, check, check.

I picture Rania's slight smile, barely visible under her hazmat suit. I picture Xander's broad smile, the clapping of his gloved hands, that thunderous sound that humans can make.

The clapping—I wish I could hear it. But I can imagine it. It makes me feel good to imagine it.

And even though I cannot hear the hazmats, I can make sure they hear me. I open my microphone and set it to record. I capture the soft whistle of Mars's wind. The low hum of my engine. The quiet that is so unlike the quiet of the laboratory. I hope they will notice that quiet. That they will understand it. I bet Rania will.

I send the recording.

MORE PICTURES

I look around. I am here. I have made it.

The command center asks for more photographs. They want to be able to pinpoint my exact location before they give me the okay to move my wheels on Mars for the first time.

I snap as many as I can.

"Do you think they will understand what it is like from the photographs?" Fly asks. He is bouncing around inside me. He is eager to move, I can tell.

"I don't know." I do know that humans perceive things differently than robots. I am only able to send them back the information that I observe. It will be their job to understand it.

A slight gust of wind ripples past me. I look at the sky again. It is turning from a reddish color to a more yellow one. I snap another picture of it. It is worthy of many, many pictures.

I use my cameras to scan the horizon. In the far distance, I spot the outline of dark mountains that exist on the rim of the crater. They tower overhead and cast their shadows across the sand. Mars has a lot of mountains. The tallest of which is named Olympus Mons. It is three times taller than the tallest mountain on Earth.

I do not believe I will get to see Olympus Mons on this mission, but I am not quite sure. I will have to do further research on that.

"What are you looking for?" Fly asks. He is able to see all the photographs I take.

"Everything," I say.

"No," he says. "What are you really looking for?"

"Dust storms," I say. It is only then that I realize that is actually what I've been scanning my surroundings for. But this seems like a rational choice. One that Journey would make. I decide to be proud of it.

"We need to be careful of them. The rover we've been sent to revive went offline because he was caught in a dust storm," I explain.

"Okay," Fly says. There is a long pause, and then he adds, "Let's not get caught in a dust storm."

"I think that is a good plan," I say.

"Avoid dust and see stars," Fly reminds me.

"Yes," I say, and I take more pictures.

Dear Res,

You landed!!! Watching you land was different than
watching you take off. I didn't even cover my eyes because
I had such a good feeling about it. I did hold my breath,
though.

And guess who I watched the landing with? ALL OF NASA!!!
Okay, maybe not ALL of NASA, but so many people were
there. We sat in this big room with this HUGE screen. Dad
held Mom's hand, and Mom held my hand, and I held Sitti's
hand as we watched you get closer and closer to Mars.
When you finally landed, the whole room erupted in cheers.
I don't think I've ever heard so much clapping.

Mom had tears in her eyes when she pulled me in for a
hug. I told her she didn't have to cry because you had
landed and that made her cry more! Moms can be so
weird.

Everyone here is totally freaking out about the
photographs you've taken. NASA was able to blow them up
and zoom in and do all this other super-scientific stuff

with them, and you know what? They're pretty confident that they know for sure—just based on your pictures!—that Mars definitely had water at some point.

That's like a HUGE discovery.

"We were right about Jezero Crater!" Mom said to Dad when she came home from work. Dad picked her up and gave her a small spin around the kitchen.

I said, "Ew, stop being gross," but really, I was super excited and happy.

Anyway, you should feel proud of yourself. I mean, your mission is off to an incredible start.

Mom says she's now hoping that you can help us to better understand what happened to Mars's water. Why did it all go away? And she's hoping to find out if anything ever lived on Mars.

That last question gives me goose bumps. Do you think you'll find any aliens? Mom says that is unlikely, but I can't stop thinking about it. Unlikely doesn't mean an absolute NO. Like something can be unlikely and still happen. OMG.

I like listening to that first recording you took. When I

listen to it, I close my eyes and pretend like I'm on Mars with you.

Your friend,

Sophie

MOVE

It finally comes. The clearance to move. The command center has determined that my landing was stable and that my wheels are not out of place. It is time to test whether I will be able to move on Mars.

"Here we go," I tell Fly.

I move forward, smoothly gliding over the sandy red ground. My wheels on the sand feel so different than they did when they moved over the floor in the lab. They sink into the ground, gripping the surface for stability.

In my rear camera, I can see the tracks I have made. The tracks that say: *I am here*.

I am a rover who has made it to Mars! And I am a rover who can rove on Mars. I take a photo of the tracks and send them to the command center.

I keep moving. The only sound around is the soft whisper of wind, but in my head, I imagine the hazmats' clapping.

"We're doing it!" Fly says.

"We're doing it," I agree.

"Now it's time to find Courage," Fly says.

"Now it's time to find a fossil," I say.

There is so much to do. There is so much to explore.

"Now it's time to get to work," Guardian says, and I feel too much of the human emotion of excitement to even be annoyed at Guardian's bossiness.

"Thank you," I say.

NIGHT AND DAY

In the laboratory, I did not truly understand the concepts of night and day.

I knew the hazmats went to a place they called home. I knew the hazmats did something they called sleep. I heard the words *night* and *day*, and I cataloged them because I am good at cataloging and learning words. But I did not quite understand the concept.

My system knows that planet Earth orbits the sun. It knows that Mars also orbits the sun. And I know that the rotation of Mars and the rotation of Earth create what hazmats call days and what hazmats call night.

I understand all of this.

But still. I was not prepared for the actuality of day and night. For the darkness. For what it is like to observe the sky fade from a dusty red to a black so dense and saturated that there is no need for me to even run the color through the pigment filter.

The darkness of the night sky is nothing like the darkness of the laboratory. Just like how the sun's light is nothing like the fluorescent lights of the laboratory.

But the most different and astounding thing is the stars.

On days when the dust is less prevalent in Mars's atmosphere, Fly and I are able to see the stars. We are able to *really* see them.

Wow was the word that filled up my whole system when I first saw the stars. But it still didn't feel big enough to express what I wanted to express.

"Wow, wow, wow." I said it three times. Hoping it would grow in size. That the word would expand to hold everything my system was processing.

"Wow, wow, wow, wow," Fly said four times, which let me know that he understood, too. That there were not enough *wow*s in the universe.

I have taken many pictures of the sky. Even though the command center did not directly request them. Somehow I know that they need to see them.

Somehow I know that when Xander sees the photographs he will say, "Wow."

EARTH

Late at night, I am able to locate a pale white dot in the sky.

It is tiny and faint. My system tells me it is approximately thirty-four million miles away.

That tiny pale white dot is Earth.

That tiny pale white dot is where Xander is. It is where Rania is. Where Journey is. Where the laboratory is. Where everything I used to know exists.

When my camera lens focuses on that tiny pale white dot, I feel so far away from them.

But I also like that I can see them.

I take a picture to send back. To send back to Earth.

"I like being here now," I say to Fly. "But someday, I know I will be the human emotion of happy to go back to Earth."

"Gruzunks," Guardian says. "I have never heard of a rover returning to Earth."

"I am going to return to Earth," I say. "I was built to return to Earth." Because I am not a hazmat and I do not speak with human speech, my voice never quivers. But if I were a hazmat, my voice would've probably quivered when I said that. Because I am not entirely certain that my return will actually occur.

"Is that correct? That you will be returning?" Guardian asks. "I do not believe I had that information."

"It is," I tell Guardian.

"If you find something worth returning you for," Fly says.

"Wait," I say. "How do you know that?"

"I listened."

"To me and Journey?"

"Yes," Fly says. "I had no choice. You were very noisy."

"You should have told us you were listening."

"Oh," Fly says. "I thought it was important to listen. So that I could know what we are searching for."

"The helicopter is indeed correct. It is important that he understands what to look for once he is in the air," Guardian says. "He will be your best tool when it comes to locating a fossil."

"And locating Courage," Fly says. "When will I get to fly?"

"When the command center desk tells us."

"It seems like it is taking a long time."

"Perhaps," I say. "But they want to make sure the conditions are right."

"Don't you want to get started?" Fly asks.

"Of course I do," I say.

"I wonder what Courage will be like."

"Me too," I say.

I am quiet for a while because I am wondering about a lot of things. I wonder if I will be able to find a fossil. If I will be able to bring Courage back online. But most of all, I can't stop staring at the tiny pale white dot that I know is Earth and wondering if Journey is sitting in the laboratory all by herself in the darkness that is so unlike the darkness of Mars at night.

You would like it here, I think. *Someday I hope I will be able to tell you about it. Though I know that when I do, you will still act like you know more about Mars than me. And that will be what humans call annoying. Because you are often annoying. But I miss you, annoyingness and all.*

In the quiet of my wondering, there is a noise. A flapping. I quickly adjust my cameras to scan all around.

"What is that?" Fly asks.

"The wind," Guardian says.

"Is it a dust devil? We really want to avoid dust devils," Fly reminds me.

"I know, Fly. I do not think it is a dust devil." I recheck my cameras. No dust devils in sight.

"I can see clearly from up here. It is not a dust devil," Guardian says. "It was most likely the wind."

"Are you sure that was the wind?" I say. I continue to survey the area. My cameras zooming in and tilting. In the darkness, I can make out the shadowy outline of the mountainous buttes that surround us. "It sounded different."

"Yes," Guardian says. "The wind often makes that sound when it comes into contact with the rock features."

As I keep scanning, I do not find anything out of the ordinary. I can't shake the feeling that that sound was something else, though. I hear Journey telling me to be rational. To let go of this feeling, of this human emotion.

But I keep wondering about it anyway.

EXPLORING

I spend the next months roving around the area where I have landed. Fly stays inside me because we have not yet been given the clearance for him to fly. He grows more and more impatient each day. It seems that Fly also shares my dislike of waiting.

"When?" he says.

"Soon," I say.

"That's what you said yesterday."

"Soon," I say again, and hope that my assessment that clearance will come soon is correct. I, of course, am eager to begin the most important part of our mission, too. To discover something that will earn us our trip back. But I keep this to myself because I do not want to make the waiting any harder for Fly.

I have been lasering the ground and analyzing minerals. I have been making small discoveries, here and there. Tiny pieces of information that I have been able to send back to the command center. But I know I was not sent here to make small discoveries.

I was sent here to do something big.

"How many more days until I fly?" Fly asks.

"I do not have a precise estimation for that," I say.

"But how do you know it will be soon, then?"

"Because it will be," I say. "Just hold on a little longer."

"That's what you said yesterday."

"And it is what I'm saying today," I say.

Tomorrow, I hope, I will have another answer. My time log tells me that it will technically be tomorrow in two hours, thirty-seven minutes, and thirty-eight seconds. Robots do not naturally understand time, but I have been equipped with a log that helps me to track it. I have learned that humans divide time into segments called years, months, and days. On Mars, days are approximately forty-one minutes longer than on Earth. I always try my best to make the most of those forty-one extra minutes.

While I wait for instructions from the command center, I continue to rove, gliding over a sand dune that is relatively easy to traverse. Beyond the horizon, jagged cliffs sprout up from the ground. I make a note to try my best to stay on this sandy path.

"Have you found a fossil yet?"

"No, Fly," I say. "Not yet."

"Do we have a specific place we should be looking for one?"

"That's what we have to figure out."

"You mean it's our job to figure out where on this whole planet we can find a fossil?"

"Don't bug out," I say as I sense Fly getting more and more jittery from his position inside me. Bugging out is what happens when a robot gets too worked up. "The hazmats chose for us to land here in Jezero Crater for a reason. They think that a long time ago there was water here. And because of the possibility that there was once water, they think fossils might exist somewhere in this crater."

"What is water?" Fly asks.

"Water is made from two parts hydrogen and one part oxygen," Guardian says.

Guardian is often silent. But sometimes she unexpectedly interrupts me and Fly's conversations. Fly does not always like Guardian's intrusions. I am not quite sure what I think of Guardian yet.

"Can you always hear us?" I ask Guardian.

"Gruzunks! Of course I can. What would be the point if I couldn't?"

"What do you mean, the point?" Fly says.

"The point," Guardian repeats. "My assignment is to guide you. To watch over you. That is only possible if I can always locate and hear you."

"Oh," Fly and I say at the same time. It makes me remember how Xander and Rania would sometimes speak at the exact same time.

"Water is important because it sustains life," I say. "And that means, we are most likely to find a fossil in a place that once had water."

"Sustains life for who? Hazmats?" Fly asks.

"Yes," Guardian says. "It is only humans that need water. I do not. Resilience does not. You do not."

I am about to comment that this is because based on the technical definition, robots are not alive. This is a fact that makes me feel an unpleasant human emotion when I think too much about it. But before I can share my issues with the technical definition of living, my thought pattern is interrupted by a sound.

That sound. The same strange sound from before.

I was wrong earlier when I said it was a flapping. As I listen more carefully, I notice it is a whirling. A long, high-pitched whistle.

"Do you hear that?" Fly says.

"It's just the wind," Guardian says.

"It is coming from a far distance," I say. "The wind sounds more constant, does it not? Less tied to a certain place?"

"Gruzunks! You are just not used to Mars yet. I assure you—it is the wind," Guardian says.

I need to be rational. I know this.

I was built to be rational.

But I keep scanning the area, searching for the source of the sound. Determined to figure out exactly what it is.

I want to believe Guardian that it is the wind, but I do not. I do not think it is the wind. I do not think so at all.

I wish I could ask someone, someone like Xander or

Rania, about it. But I cannot. So instead, I use my microphone. I make a recording, and I send it back to the command center. I hope Xander and Rania will know what I am asking: *Is this the wind?*

Dear Resilience,

Are you getting used to Mars? You've been there for a while now. Do you feel alone? Or do you like having all that space to yourself?

I started school again. I'm in eighth grade now. Summer went so fast. Is it summer on Mars? I should probably know that. I guess I could ask Mom. I remember she once told me that the average temperature on Mars is around −81 degrees, so it's hard to imagine that it ever feels like summer there. I mean, I know it doesn't FEEL like summer, but I'm asking if it's the season of summer. . . . I'm going to stop talking about this now. My friend Immani would say, "Sophie, you're being so awkward!"

Immani says that to me all the time now. I guess I am kind of awkward. But I'm also still her best friend. And it doesn't make me feel great when she says that. You know how it makes me feel? Like I'm on a totally different planet than her. Get it?

Okay, fine. That probably wasn't as funny as I wanted it to be. Anyway, I bet your drone helicopter never tells you that you're being awkward. That's a real lucky thing, let me tell you. I'm excited for your drone helicopter to fly. Mom says that is going to happen soon.

I keep listening to that new recording on Mars that you took. NASA says they hear a sound in it that they can't detect. I can't stop wondering about what it is. I asked Mom if she thought it could be an alien. She just laughed. But that's not a no!

I hope if you meet an alien that they turn out to be nice. Nicer than Immani is being anyway.

I think Mom and Dad can tell I'm having a rough time in eighth grade. Dad told me that no one likes junior high. But I don't think that's true. Other people seem to be having fun. They're always laughing and stuff in the hallway. Mom says I need to find my people, but I don't know what that means exactly. Like I thought my best friend was my people?

I stopped playing soccer, which Mom and Dad aren't thrilled about, but I didn't want to do it anymore. I don't know why. I'm just not into it. I'm thinking of joining the school newspaper, though. I like writing to you, so maybe I'd like that.

Okay, I'm going to try to go back to bed now.

Your friend,

Sophie

ROVING

The command desk does not say anything about the recording I sent. I do not know if this means they think it was only wind or if they are investigating further.

I often hear the sound in the distance. Whenever I hear it, I tell myself: *Be rational. You were sent here to be rational. It is only the wind.*

Sometimes I am able to believe that. Other times, I don't.

I spend my days exploring and waiting for news from the command center that Fly is cleared to take flight so that we can begin the bigger parts of my mission.

Some days, it is easier to wait than others. Some days, it is easier to ignore the sound than other days.

I rove over the sand. I take pictures of my tracks. I listen for that sound.

I rove and I rove and I rove.

FLIGHT

I am thinking about the sound that I do not believe is the wind when I receive news from the command desk about Fly. The time has come for us to prepare for his first flight.

I was roving over uneven ground when I got the message, and the excitement of getting the message while climbing the rocky ground caused me to wobble slightly. I am still getting used to traversing the dips and crevices of Mars's surface. Each roll of my wheels is a surprise. Occasionally I find myself teetering when I do not expect it, but so far my wheels have been able to grip and keep me upright.

No falls yet.

"You will need to find somewhere flat with easy terrain. That would be the most appropriate spot for Fly to attempt his first flight. Where you are right now is not a good place."

"I know," I say. Guardian is always telling me what to do. Sometimes I find this to be quite irritating.

"I'm ready, Res!" Fly says. He is buzzing inside me. "Let's go find Courage! I sure hope he's nice."

"Gruzunks! Nice? What is nice?" Guardian says.

"Friendly," Fly explains. "I hope he likes questions."

"He is not online. Which means he is neither friendly nor nice."

"Ha! I got you to say *friendly* and *nice*. You used human words," Fly says.

"Gruzunks! Please take this mission seriously."

"I'm serious!" Fly says. "I am the most serious you could seriously be!"

"Helicopter! Please just stop!" Guardian says.

"Okay," Fly says. There is a long pause, and then he says, "But seriously, can I fly yet?"

I picture Xander. I imagine his voice. I say to Fly, "It's almost time, buddy."

HOPEFULLY

Even though it is annoying how many instructions Guardian gives, she turns out to be very helpful in leading me to a spot that will be good for Fly's first flight.

The spot Guardian found is flat and a safe area, free from obstacles such as mountainous buttes or large boulders. But it is quite a far distance away, and it will take me a while to reach it.

"Please speed up if possible," Guardian says. "We want to be as efficient as we can be."

"I'm roving as fast I can," I say as my wheels bump over sandy rock.

The purpose of Fly's flight is to collect new data in a quicker and more efficient fashion than I am able to. He will be able to gather aerial footage of Mars's surface. This footage will be sent back to the command center, and they will study it. If they notice something interesting, they will instruct us to move in the direction of it in order to be able to further investigate it. I also will be able to view the footage and it will help me to make my own decisions as well.

"Maybe this is a good spot?" Fly asks. "Or this one? What do you think, Res? Huh, huh? What do you think?"

"We are almost to the spot Guardian found, Fly. I'm following the coordinates Guardian sent."

"But why not this spot? This spot seems fine."

"Helicopter, please be quiet."

"My name is Fly."

"Be quiet," Guardian says.

"You are pretty mean," Fly says. "Weren't you programmed to be nicer?"

"*Mean* and *nice* are human words. I was programmed to be efficient," Guardian says.

"Efficient," Fly says.

"Yes, efficient. Speaking of which, Resilience, please keep moving. My own time log tells me we are behind schedule."

"I'm roving as fast as I can," I say again.

"Why do we need the ground to be flat?" Fly asks. By my calculations, Fly has managed to ask ten questions in less than the span of one human minute. This is quite impressive. Guardian would probably say it is quite something else.

I do not always have the answers to Fly's questions. Guardian always answers, but I am starting to understand that answering is not necessarily the same thing as knowing the answer.

"Because if something goes wrong during the flight, we want you to land in a place that is easily accessible for Resilience to retrieve you," Guardian says, answering Fly's question again.

"Res, is something going to go wrong?" Fly asks.

I want to say no. I want to make Fly feel better. But I don't know the answer. "I will make sure to retrieve you no matter what."

"Most likely you will complete your mission without incident and Resilience will not need to retrieve you."

"Hopefully," Fly says.

"Gruzunks! *Hopefully* is not a word that registers with me," Guardian says.

"It registers with me," I admit, and then repeat, "Hopefully." After I say it, I consider that it may have been a mistake to share that information with Guardian. *Hopefully* it was not.

"Hopefully," Fly says again.

"You two are quite a pair," Guardian says.

"Beeps and boops. Is that a positive statement or a negative one?" I ask.

"I do not know," Guardian says.

For once, Guardian does not know the answer. But I think I do.

FIRST FLIGHT

I reach the spot Guardian selected. After doing a thorough scan, I determine that Guardian was indeed correct that this is an ideal location for Fly's first flight.

"Thank you, Guardian. This is a good spot," I say.

"I know," Guardian says. "I am very skilled at my job."

"Okay," I say to Fly. "It is time to come out."

"Are you sure?"

"Certain," I say.

"You need to listen to Resilience, Helicopter. Resilience is in charge," Guardian says. "You should not second-guess Resilience's commands."

"Zappedty zip," I say. "I am not in charge. I am not giving commands. Fly and I are a team. Actually, you, Fly, and me are a team."

"Zappedty zip?" Fly says. "I have never heard you say that."

"I made it up," I say. "I created it." If I had a hazmat voice, Fly would be able to hear the human emotion of pride in my voice. "Do you like it?'

As much as I like saying *beeps and boops*, it is Journey's phrase. Journey is the one that came up with it. And I've decided that I needed to make up my own combination of words because I am the one here.

I'm the rover on Mars.

And I am the one Fly needs to support him right now on his flight.

"I really do, Res," Fly says. "Zappedty zip."

Fly pops out from inside me. He flutters in the air, just at the edge of what I can see with my camera lens.

"Wait," I tell Fly. "Don't go yet. We need permission from the command center."

I wait for the instructions to come. It is a long wait. Fly hovers low in the air, right above the flat sand. The sun is beaming down from the sky, casting slanted light across the red sand. The wind in this spot is calm and low. It does not make any loud whooshing sounds. I listen for that one particular sound, but I do not hear it.

Finally, the message we have been waiting for comes. "We have been given the go," I say.

"Now?" Fly says, and even though he is speaking to me in machine code language, I can tell he is the human emotion of nervous. I think of Xander's dark circles. But then I think of Rania's one special song. I try to hum it, but I am not as good at singing as Fly is.

"That is a nice song. I have never heard it before."

"A friend once shared it with me. I thought you would like if I shared it with you," I say.

I expect Guardian to interject, but she does not. She lets me keep humming.

"Thanks, Res," Fly says. "I'm ready now."

"You were made to do this, Fly."

He hovers in the air, and then he goes up and up and up. He zooms over the flat expanse. I record Fly in flight, and from my camera's vantage point, Fly is becoming a smaller and smaller dot on the horizon. On another camera, I am able to see what he sees. Even though we are not together, I am still connected with Fly.

"Do you see that?" Fly says over and over again. His video is clear and steady. I can tell he feels comfortable in the air.

"Yes," I say, again and again. "I'm seeing all of it."

Today the sky is a light yellow. The sand beneath it is full of red and brown pigments. Our system will alert us to any particular part of the ground that may contain minerals or rocks of special interest. Rocks that could contain clues to whether this planet ever had water. If it ever had life.

I think of how Journey told me that what Rania really wants is for me to find a fossil.

I'm searching, Rania, I think. *I will find one for you.*

"Res!" Fly shouts. "Look!"

I watch the camera. The one that shows me the world through Fly's perspective. Fly has spotted another rover.

Fly has found Courage.

A PLAN

"That was a highly successful first flight, Helicopter," Guardian says. "You have found the offline rover."

"Yes," I say. "Great job, Fly."

Fly flies back inside me. I replay the footage of his flight. I study the aerial footage from the moment Fly discovered Courage. The rover is stranded in the middle of a sand dune. The terrain does not appear to be particularly difficult, but the rover is completely motionless. I know that Rania and Xander explained to me that Courage went offline during a dust storm, but it makes me feel the human emotion of worried to see him motionless on a stretch of ground that should not have caused him difficulty.

There is red and brown dirt caked all over the rover. And worse, it looks like at least two of his six wheels are missing. This will make movement very difficult when we bring him back online.

"Guardian, was Courage taken by surprise by the dust storm?"

"Oh, yes," Guardian says. "It came out of nowhere. That happens sometimes. Courage was an excellent rover, but that storm was his demise. That is the way of rovers, though. You are not meant to last forever."

I replay Guardian's sentence through my system: *You are not meant to last forever.*

"But I am meant to return to Earth," I say.

"You keep saying that, but I am not sure of the validity of that statement."

I know that I am correct. Xander and Rania were clear that if I did well on my mission, if I found something worth bringing back to Earth, that I would get to return.

And maybe, just maybe, somewhere in Courage's system there is something that falls into that category of worthiness. There is a chance Courage collected a particularly interesting rock sample. And there is an even better chance that Courage captured valuable footage of the dust storm.

I experience the human emotion of hope. It is a sticky and strange feeling. It is a beautiful one.

"I need to make my way to Courage to bring him online," I say.

"Yes," Guardian says. "I do agree with that."

I replay Fly's footage again. I have sent it to the command center. I have not yet received a response, but that is not abnormal. There is usually a long lag. It is also possible that most of the hazmats are performing the action they call sleep.

"Is that area prone to dust storms?" I ask.

"A dust storm can occur anywhere," Guardian says. "You should know that."

"I do, but I was asking for clarification."

"I don't want to get caught in a dust storm," Fly says.

"Me either, buddy."

"Then you must always be alert," Guardian says.

I listen to the wind blowing. It is picking up speed. I use my cameras to scan the area. I do not see anything that is particularly alarming.

"I will be alert."

"Promise, Res?" Fly says.

"I promise. Now, let's go find Courage," I say.

I set my wheels in motion. It is time for me to do something big.

It is time for me to earn my return to Earth.

PART FOUR
OUR MISSION

FORWARD

With Fly's footage and Guardian's help, I am able to approximate the location of Courage. Fly is back inside my chamber, but I will frequently ask him to go out and do an aerial survey of the area to make sure we are headed in the right direction.

I move much slower than Fly, but he is patient with me. He never tells me to speed up. It will take me many human months, longer than a human year to reach Courage. But Fly does not make me feel bad about my speed in comparison to his. He knows that we were built differently for a reason.

Guardian, though, is constantly telling me to hurry while also reminding me that I cannot forget my other mission tasks, like collecting samples from the terrain. When Guardian reminds me of the other part of my mission, I think about what Rania said in the lab on one of the very last nights. How she was worried that the hazmats were asking too much of me.

I can do it, I say to myself, pretending I am speaking to Rania. *You built me for this.*

Five human months into the trek to find Courage, just when I am feeling good about the job I am doing, Guardian says, "Gruzunks, are you sure you haven't received a message from the command center that you are behind schedule?"

"No," I say. "I have not." I do not say: *You are annoying sometimes*. But I think it. Then I try to think a nice thought, too: *You are helpful sometimes*. This is what I believe the hazmats call balance.

"You should trust Res. He is doing a good job," Fly says.

"Gruzunks! Trust? That is human nonsense. I am just asking Resilience to do his job."

"He is doing his job!" Fly says. "And he's doing it well!"

"No one asked you, Helicopter."

I let Fly and Guardian argue for a bit while I make sure to carefully study the ground that I am roving over. I stop to laser a patch of ground.

So far while on Mars, after reading the results from my laser, I have occasionally chosen to drill down into the ground to gather a soil sample. And after collecting the soil sample, I conducted a thorough analysis of it in my chemical laboratory.

The findings have been quite expected. To my disappointment. Nothing out of the ordinary. Nothing that would make Xander say, "Wow."

And while I have collected several soil samples, I have not yet collected a rock sample. I only have a limited amount of room in my laboratory chamber, so I have to be judicious about what samples I collect.

I keep finding samples that primarily contain silicon or aluminum or magnesium. I would like to find something that contains salt. If it contains salt, it is possible that the salt is left over from ancient water. Also, salt often can act like a time capsule, preserving signs of life from long ago. Which means if the rock shows signs of salt, there is a theoretical chance that there could be a fossil inside it. But I have not yet found any signs of salt. Or anything that is carbon-based—another strong sign of ancient life.

I must keep searching.

Whenever I make the choice not to collect a sample, I miss Journey. I find it frustrating, this missing feeling. But even if I don't want to feel it, I do. It lingers in my system and refuses to leave.

Despite not wanting to, I find myself wondering about Journey and what choices she would make about the rock and soil samples if she were here. Wondering if somehow her choices would be more rational.

I am trying my best to be rational, but I sometimes have doubts that I am doing a good job at it. Journey would probably say that the fact I am using the human word *doubt* is a clear sign that I have a problem.

"Are you making sure to use your X-ray tool?" Guardian asks.

For Guardian's information, I have used my X-ray tool twelve times so far to better see and analyze the insides of rocks. But I do not give her the precise numbers. Instead, I say, "Don't you think I would have let you know if I found something that is obviously a fossil?"

"I am just checking. My job is to check."

"And my job is to rove," I say. I x-ray the ground just to show Guardian. I know there is nothing of interest there, but I want to show her that I can do it.

The sky overhead is a pale gray. The sun is rising, casting a greenish light. Mars, I have learned, has many skies. Sometimes the sun can feel warm—bright and yellow. And other times, it takes on this other quality that makes the inside of my system feel uneasy. I snap a picture of this odd greenish light.

"You should let Res do his job. He is doing a good job," Fly says.

"I am doing my best," I say.

I am trying. I am roving.

Dear Res,

I've never seen Mom more excited than the day she came home from work and told me that you had found the other rover! That was a really good day. It's been a while since I've had that good of a day.

But I guess there are a few other good things I can tell you about. For starters, I'm writing for the school newspaper now. I've made some new friends who also write for the paper. I really like Maggie and Sana. You'd probably like them, too.

I'm almost done with eighth grade. That means I'll be in high school next year. I'm a little nervous about it. Things are still weird with Immani. We hardly ever talk anymore. Sitti says it's normal to grow apart from friends when you get older, but I don't know. Do you think you'll ever grow apart from your drone? It's probably ridiculous to ask you that, but I feel like you'd have a good answer. You seem very smart. I mean, look—you already found the other rover!

I think Mom is prouder of you for that than she'll ever be of me. Wait, that came out wrong. That makes it seem like I'm jealous of you or mad—and I'm not. I promise. I just feel weird and kind of grouchy a lot recently. I don't know why.

Mom and Dad keep whispering about something at night. And Mom seems REALLY tired all the time. I mean, I know you've been on Mars for almost two years now, and she'd been working on you for like a billion years before that, but still. She just looks . . . different. I don't really know how to describe it.

It makes me a little scared. Which makes it hard to sleep. Which I guess is why I'm writing to you again. Do you think I'm too old now to write to you?

Your friend,

Sophie

ROVING, PART TWO

I rove. And I rove. And I rove.

The expanse in front of me appears endless. The scenery has been steadily the same. Sand to all sides, occasionally a scattering of boulders or the briefest silhouette of jagged mountains in the far-off distance. Only the sky changes, cycling through all of its colors and shades.

The wind ripples across the sand. Sometimes it sounds like a whisper, and sometimes it is so loud that it makes the inside of my system rattle.

Once in a while, I will say to Fly, "Do you hear that?"

It is the sound again. The whirling one, the one almost like a human whistle. The one that I cannot place.

"Yes," Fly says.

"It is the wind," Guardian says. Again.

And I say what I always say: "But it sounds different than the wind."

I take another recording of it. I send it back to the command desk. They do not respond. I wish I had the ability to ask them why.

Do you hear what I hear? I want to say. *What do you think?*

It is quite frustrating to have so many questions and no way to ask them.

"I don't think it is much farther," Fly says.

I replay the video I took of Fly's flight. He is somewhat correct. We have made good progress. We have been roving for over one full human year, but there is still much distance to be traveled.

"We're getting there," I say.

For most of the journey, the ground has been more sand than rock, but then, abruptly, the ground beneath turns rougher. And steeper. My wheels bounce up and down. The bouncing shakes up my whole system. My suspension goes tense. I think of the word Guardian used earlier—tired.

I feel it deep in the axis of my wheels.

But I once heard Xander say something like the only way through is forward. And so I keep moving. Forward.

My wheels let out a groan. Fly must hear the tired sound because he says, "Should I sing?"

"That would be nice," Guardian says before I can answer.

This response from Guardian gives me the human emotion of surprise. I think I like being surprised.

"I only know one song," Fly says.

"That's okay. It is a good one," I say, and remember the way Rania's voice sounded, all warm and fuzzy, when she sang into the phone for Lovebug.

I decide to share this memory with Fly. "Did you know that song is for Lovebug?"

"What is Lovebug?"

"A small hazmat who Rania loves."

"Hm. Loves? Love. Bug," Fly says. "But what does that mean? I am familiar with the concept of bugging out, but I do not think I have heard the word *love* before."

"I am not quite sure. But I think *love* is a word that humans use to indicate something that they care a lot about."

"Oh. It is a very nice word."

"Yes."

"Well, I really like Lovebug's song," Fly says.

"Me too."

"*Twinkle, twinkle,*" Fly says.

He sings for a while. Then he says, "Hmm, hmm, hmm. Maybe I will make up a new song."

"You will have lots of time to do it. Resilience still has a while to go," Guardian says.

"I know, I know," I say, my wheels grumbling beneath me. Bump, bump, bump. "I'm moving as fast as I can."

But suddenly, I no longer am able to bump, bump, bump. My system fills up with a squealing noise. Guardian says something else, but I am too distracted by a loud squeal to process what it is.

My movement grinds to a halt. There is a sputtering sound, a loud groan of my wheels. I try to move, but I can't.

My wheels squeal-groan again. Louder this time. They sound angry.

"What is that?" Fly asks.

I try to press forward. My wheels spin. I do not move. This is like the test that was done in the laboratory. But this time Xander and Rania are not here to fix it for me.

I try my wheels again.

Spin, spin, spin. Squeal, squeal, squeal.

I do not move. I am stuck.

We are stuck.

"We're not moving," Fly says.

"That is an obvious fact. You do not need to state it," Guardian says.

"Something is wrong," I say.

"Gruzunks! That is another obvious fact."

"Zappedty, zip. I know, I know," I say.

I run a system check. A laser shoots out to study the mineral makeup of the ground around me. The dirt appears to have particles of the elements iron, magnesium, and silicon. There is nothing unusual about this. The only thing unusual about this stretch of ground is a rough consistency. But my wheels should be able to manage it.

This is not expected. I am not sure I am good at things that are not expected.

The hazmat word *worry* enters my system. The roar of the wind is growing stronger.

"Be rational, Res," I say to myself. "Be. Rational."

The wind continues to whip around me, flinging up sand and dirt.

"Do you see any dust devils?" I ask Guardian at the same time I scan the peripheral area with my camera. "Oh no," I say. "I see one. It is far away now, but if we stay stuck . . ."

"If we stay stuck, it will get us!" Fly says.

"I know, Fly. I'm going to do my best, but . . ."

Guardian must sense my waves of concern because she says, "You were built to be able to handle this, Resilience. Run through your system's instructions. You can get yourself unstuck."

It is the nicest thing Guardian has ever said to me. Guardian's kindness makes me think of Xander. I hear Xander's words in my head. Telling me the meaning of my name. Resilience.

I must earn my name.

I must earn it over and over again.

"You are correct," I tell Guardian. "I will fix this."

"Yes, you will, Res!" Fly says. But it comes out more like a song. A new song.

PROBLEM-SOLVING

"We did not anticipate this problem," I say.

"I did not think the terrain got this rough," Fly says.

I replay Fly's footage. Now that I know what to look for, I am able to see the problem that I missed the first time— the unexpected increase in the steepness of the slope of the ground. I would like to be able to express the human emotion of frustration. But I cannot.

I am stuck.

I beam my laser down onto the soil again. The calculations are very similar to the first time. Again, there is nothing that stands out as being the cause of the problem. Even with the sharp incline, it should be possible for my wheels to move. I was built to be able to scale hills. So why can't I rove?

"What are you looking for?" Fly asks.

I do not respond. I keep shifting through the data I collected, searching for a pattern that will explain why I am stuck.

"Why are we stuck?" Fly asks. "Do you know yet?"

I scan the data again. I do not think I am missing anything.

"Res? What's going on?" Fly says.

"Gruzunks! Would you be quiet for a moment? Resilience is most likely working through a complicated set of calculations," Guardian says.

I am not working through a complicated set of calculations. It would be good if I were because it would mean I knew what was wrong. But I still can't figure it out.

"Guardian, have you received any messages from back on Earth?"

"That's a negative," Guardian answers.

My wheels splutter again. I push as hard as I can, and there is a loud grinding sound. It sounds absolutely terrible. It is my least favorite sound in the whole universe. I am making that declaration even though my sample size is still very small.

I would very much like to increase my sample size, though. I would like to hear all the sounds I possibly can. But that will not happen if I stay stuck. I grind my wheels one more time. Still no movement.

"I would advise stopping that behavior," Guardian says. "You may unintentionally cause more damage to your system."

"My system is not currently damaged," I respond back quickly.

"I meant your outer shell. Or your wheels."

"I do not detect any damage to my wheels." I try to move

197

my wheels once more and hear an awful grinding sound that gives a different answer.

"Very well. You should be moving in no time, then," Guardian answers.

"Wait. Do you have a message that tells you that there is damage to my system?" I ask.

"Will one of you PLEASE tell me what is going on?" Fly says. "I'm starting to . . . bug out!"

"Is your system malfunctioning?" Guardian asks Fly at the exact same moment I say, "You are fine, Fly. It will be okay. Just give me approximately one minute and three seconds to reanalyze my system's data."

"Approximately? Any chance it will be quicker? One minute and three seconds is a really long time!" Fly says.

"Fly, please give me an affirmative or negative on if your system is really having an issue," Guardian says.

I think this is the first time Guardian has ever called Fly by his name. I consider bringing attention to this, but given all the problems facing us, I decide to hold on to this information to discuss later.

"Fly's system is fine," I clarify for Guardian. I do quickly check Fly's system before making this proclamation, but I am pleased to say my initial assessment of the situation was correct. Drones, I have learned from spending time with Fly—my sample size of one—are prone to exaggeration. "I believe Fly means that he is simply feeling out of sorts because we are stuck."

"Gruzunks! Believe? Feel—" Guardian begins to say.

"We know," I say. "Let's table that disagreement for now and focus on the problem at hand."

That last thing is something I once heard Rania say to Xander. I remember the day she said it. It was a day when there was something very, very wrong with the landing calculation. Xander had then become concerned about something with my camera angle capabilities. Rania had acknowledged that it could potentially be a problem, but she hadn't wanted one problem to distract from the ability to solve the landing calculation problem.

I still do not have a message from the command center.

"We should receive a message from the command center soon, right?" I ask Guardian.

Come on, Rania, I think. *Come on, Xander. I am counting on you to help me. We are a team. Aren't we?*

"Perhaps," Guardian says. "Not always. If there is nothing drastically wrong with your system, then this is a routine problem. Rovers are expected to solve routine problems."

"But I don't know if I can."

Maybe rational rovers like Journey can solve routine problems. But I feel the human emotion of doubt winding its way through my system, snaking into my wiring and dripping down into the core of my battery.

The hazmats sent the wrong rover, I think.

And because they sent the wrong rover, we are stuck. The mission is stuck.

"You can do this, Res," Fly says. I have sensed Fly jittering around inside me. He is not literally having technical system issues, but he is clearly in distress.

"Could I help?" Fly suggests.

"I'm not sure. . . ."

"I could do a quick flight and scan the area. Maybe there is something you aren't seeing," Fly says.

"I don't see anything from way up here, but Fly could get a more detailed look," Guardian inputs.

"What do you think, Res?" Fly asks.

I am unsure. There is a chance Fly could be helpful, but I also don't want to put Fly in any unnecessary danger.

"I think I should do it! I'm going to do it!" Fly says, and before I've responded, Fly has already sputtered out from inside me and is darting off ahead. "Just hold on, Res! I'll let you know if I see anything."

"Fly, please be safe."

"I'm fine!"

"And, Fly?"

"Yes?"

"Thank you," I say.

A SOLUTION

The positive is that Fly returns unharmed. The negative is that Fly's flight does not detect anything that even hints as to why my wheels are stuck.

Using my cameras and navigation tools, I track that the dust storm is getting closer to us.

"Do you see that?" Fly asks.

"We all see it," Guardian says. "It is nothing to worry about it. It is far away."

"But—" Fly says.

"It is still far away," Guardian repeats.

I imagine the dust storm getting closer. I imagine waves of dirt rising up from the ground, burying Fly and me. I imagine ending up just like Courage.

I try to move my wheels again. My wheels make the horrible grinding sound. I do not move.

"Get away from it, Res!" Fly says.

"We are away from it."

"But—" Fly says. He jitters around inside me.

"It is far away," Guardian repeats one more time.

I use my system to measure the distance. Guardian is correct: it is still far away. But it is quickly moving in our direction. I do not share this information with Fly.

"Have you tried a circle?" Guardian asks.

"A circle?"

"Yes. Moving in a circle."

"I can't move at all."

"You can't move forward or backward. But have you tried moving to the side?"

It occurs to me then that I have not. I am not sure why.

Bracing for the grinding sound again, I ask my wheels to move to the side. There is a whirling, a spit-up of sand, but I move! My one wheel comes unstuck, then another. Soon, I am really moving.

"Hey!" I say. "It worked!"

"I thought it would."

"I don't know why I didn't think of it."

"That's why I'm here," Guardian says.

"I'm glad you are," I say.

FORWARD AGAIN

I move horizontally for a moment, and then I stop.

"It's probably time to try and move forward," Fly says. "To get away from the dust storm."

"Gruzunks! There is no probably about it. It is certainly time. Move forward, Resilience," says Guardian.

Slowly, my wheels roll forward. It works! I steer us on a route that falls way outside the trajectory of the dust storm. I pretend I hear Xander in my head saying, *That's it, buddy. Good job.*

"*Here we go,*" sings Fly.

"That's a pretty nice tune," says Guardian.

"You really think so?" Fly asks, but doesn't wait for Guardian's response and keeps singing. "*Here we go, here we go, here we go,*" Fly sings.

I agree. It is a nice tune.

The sky is darkening, but I will keep moving. Unlike the hazmats, my movements do not depend on whether or not the sun is lighting up the sky. I do take rests sometimes, though. Rests are necessary to charge my battery. But I have been told—and Guardian has confirmed—I am the most active rover that has ever been sent to Mars.

But now is certainly not the time for rest. Now is the time to move. To get us away from this dust storm.

"You're doing a good job, Resilience," Guardian says.

"But I didn't solve the problem."

"Yes, you did."

"No. You told me what to do."

"We worked together. The problem is solved. I am pleased with the outcome. You should be, too."

"Okay," I say. And I want a word like *pleased* to enter my system, but it is taking a while. I am still consumed with the worry I felt when I was stuck. It was not enjoyable to feel so helpless. It was not enjoyable at all.

My camera lens tilts toward the stars. Every night, the visibility is different. Sometimes it is like I can see the whole universe. Other times, I can barely make out anything because of the dust.

Tonight the stars are clear and bright. The sky is so beautiful that for a moment I forget all about how I got stuck.

I stare at the stars and wonder.

"Do you think there are other rovers out there?" I ask Fly.

"I don't know," Fly says.

I angle my camera to try to find the pale white dot of Earth. I am not able to find it tonight. "I wonder what Journey is doing back at the laboratory."

"Me too," Fly says. "Hey, Res?"

"Yeah?"

"You wonder about a lot of things, don't you?"

"I guess I do."

"I like that. I like to wonder with you."

"I like that you like to wonder with me, too, Fly," I say.

I snap a picture of the night sky. The command desk has not requested a photograph, but I want to take one.

I would like them to see what I see. I would like them to wonder.

I send it.

THE ROCK FORMATION

On the footage from Fly's most recent flight, I notice a maze of boulders that are arranged in a unique pattern. The boulders make a winding path to one giant mesa, a large hill with a flat top. There is a tunnel-like opening on the right side of the mesa, about halfway up. To reach that opening, I would have to scale the rocky slope. This would be a difficult task. But if I were able to do that, I just might be able to get inside. My system spikes with curiosity.

I replay the footage again. "Do you see that?" I ask Fly.

He can watch the video of his flight at the same time as me on his own system.

"Yes, yes," Fly says. "But wait, the terrain looks particularly hazardous, don't you think?"

"I think we need to go investigate it," I say.

"What are you talking about?" Guardian says from overhead. Guardian cannot see the footage, so she has no way of knowing how promising this rock formation looks. That is why it is my job to narrate to her the information we have on the ground—so then she will be able to make better calculations to advise us.

"Fly has located a place of significant interest. The

ground looks markedly different from here. It stands to reason that we could find a sample that contains signs of an ancient water supply there."

I don't say that maybe inside that tunnel there is a fossil. But I have the human emotion of hope inside me. And I'm finding it very difficult to ignore this very unshakable but wonderful human emotion.

"Is that so?" Guardian says. "And you think it is worth taking a detour from your current mission to pursue this?"

"Eek, eek—I'm not sure," Fly says. "I actually wasn't looking for a place of interest. I was scanning the area for dust storms for us and looking for a way to get you unstuck. I don't think going to a place where you are more likely to get stuck is such a good idea. It also would be a very long detour."

"Zappedty zip," I say. "The very reason it is worth exploring is because the ground is different. Even from the grainy footage, I can tell that the pigments of red are significantly different than the red on the ground in the area we are presently in."

"Are you certain?" Guardian says.

I replay the footage for the twenty-ninth time. "I cannot be certain. The footage is too grainy."

"Okay, okay," Fly says. "I know the footage is a bit grainy, but I wasn't exactly trying to focus on that rock formation. I was trying—"

"We know, Fly," Guardian says. "No one is criticizing your footage."

"Hey! You're using my name now," Fly says.

"Gruzunks! Don't make me regret it. Resilience, how do you want to proceed?"

Far off in the distance, I hear that sound again. The one that Guardian is certain is the wind, but I am not so sure.

I can sense that I am close to something worthwhile. I don't know how I know that, but I just do. This is another strange but persistent feeling.

I think of Xander's gloved hand on the top of my computer brain. I think of how on that last night Rania talked to me, really talked to me. I think of how sometimes you feel something before you understand it.

"We must investigate that rock formation. I was sent here to explore all places of possible interest," I say. "No matter how dangerous."

"Okay. You are correct. That is your mission," Guardian says. "I suppose that settles it. You can pursue the detour."

"Are you sure, Res?" Fly says.

"Zappedty zip," I say. "Let's go."

Dear Res,

I know I haven't written in a while. It's been months. I wish
I could say it's because I've been busy with high school,
which is true, but it's not the whole truth. I'm not sure
your robot brain would like that idea: that something can
be true, but not be the truth.

Mom is sick.

Writing that sentence makes me feel terrible.

No one knows what it is yet. The doctors are running lots
of tests. Mom and Dad whisper at night when they think I'm
asleep. I wish someone would tell me what's really going on.

I don't know what is going to happen. Sitti wants Mom to
take a break from work, to focus on getting better. But
Mom doesn't want to. And Dad says we should support
Mom in whatever she wants to do.

Mom keeps talking about how everyone at NASA isn't sure
why you are roving down some alternative path, but how

excited she is that you're thinking for yourself. It seems like everyone else is wondering what you're doing, but Mom is totally fine just waiting to see. She trusts you.

Mom could be really sick, but at least she trusts you? Is that supposed to make me feel better somehow? She loves to tell me how proud she is of you, and I don't know what I'm supposed to do with that. It all kind of makes me mad. Like really mad. And I don't like being mad at you. Or Mom.

I guess I'm just mad at the world.

Your friend,

Sophie

A DANGEROUS FLIGHT

The journey to the odd-looking rock formation that Fly spotted during his flight takes much longer than expected. We had to select an even more inefficient route in order to avoid other dust storms. And my wheels have not been able to move very quickly, as the ground has grown more and more difficult to traverse.

I have never understood the word *tired* more than now.

Worse, the terrain is becoming even tougher as we get closer and closer to the maze of boulders. My wheels strain to grip the earth, and my system rattles as the ride becomes bumpier.

"Don't you think this is close enough, Res?" Fly says. We can see the boulders up ahead.

"You are putting wear on your system," Guardian says.

"I know," I say. I can feel the strain on my wheels, the fact that they spin with less ease than before. And I can sense the dust collecting on my outer shell. "But I am here to do a job."

"Yes, you are correct," Guardian says.

"Please be careful, Res," Fly says.

I swerve slightly to the right to avoid a series of large,

jagged rocks that poke out from the sand. We are nearing the first boulder in the formation. The mesa with the tunnel opening is still miles and miles away, though. I press forward, but my wheels make a sputtering noise.

Not again.

I push forward. Another sputtering noise. But at least I move.

"Res!" Fly says.

"Res," Guardian repeats.

"I want to go to the tunnel," I say.

"I do not know what tunnel you speak of," Guardian says.

"When Fly took the footage before, there appeared to be a large mesa with a tunnel-like opening at the end of the boulder maze."

"Why don't you have Fly take another flight?"

"But . . ." I pause. My cameras survey the area. I note the various rock formations jutting out from the ground. Their sharp and ragged edges. The unpredictable pattern of how they are arranged. The wind whips around us, making a howling noise and kicking up dust.

"I do not know if this area is the best for a flight. It seems unsafe," I finally say.

"I can do it, Res," Fly says.

"I concur with Fly," Guardian says. "While the wind conditions do not seem optimal, neither does the terrain for ground travel. It is important to get more information before you proceed."

Fly pops out from inside me. Immediately, his body sways in the wind. He eventually regains balance, but watching Fly unsteadily flap in the wind gives me the human emotion of nervous. A message from the command center appears.

"The command center wants us to proceed with caution," I say.

"Res, what does that mean?" Fly asks. He is on the ground. He looks very tiny when he is on the ground and not in flight. The wind keeps pushing at him, causing his body to rock back and forth.

"They are confirming your calculations, Guardian. They say the conditions are not optimal for flight."

"Have they forbidden it?" Guardian asks.

"No."

"Then it is your decision."

"My decision?"

That awful human feeling of nervousness grows inside my system. I call up a memory of Journey. It is easy for me to do. But my excellent memory does not mean that I know what Journey would do in this situation.

I wish I did.

"Yes. It is your call," Guardian confirms.

That strange sound echoes in the distance again. I listen carefully. It could be the wind, I guess. But there is a tonal quality that is different.

That tonal quality calls to me. I want to chase it. I want to explore.

I search my system and replay the original footage from Fly's earlier flight. It is so grainy that it is unclear exactly what the terrain is like around the mesa. It is also unclear whether or not I would even be able to access that tunnel-like opening.

It would be helpful to get more data.

"Please let me try, Res," Fly says.

"I don't know," I say.

"You said this was important. I want to help. We are a team."

Before I can answer, Fly is in the air. He takes off. The wind pushes against him, making him tilt, but he manages to regain his balance. The footage he is getting is very informative.

We were right that this ground is much different—more rock than sand. That is abundantly clear. It also looks like there is a traversable path for me to take through the rock formation toward the mesa. I am so focused on plotting out this path that I do not immediately notice the change in the condition of the wind.

"Resilience," Guardian says. "Dust devil alert! Dust devil alert! You need to pull Fly out of the air and get him back inside your chambers."

The wind picks up speed. It is all happening so fast. Dust

lifts off the ground and spins around in the air. Visibility is getting worse and worse. All I see are swirls of reddish brown. On Fly's camera, I see that his visibility is even worse than that of my cameras.

"Fly!" I say. "Come back!"

I press forward on my wheels. They make a loud screeching noise as I grind my way forward, racing to get Fly.

But it is too late. And I am too slow. The dust has risen up and formed a wind funnel. A dust devil.

The dust devil twists on the ground, careening toward Fly.

"Fly!" I say.

I keep watching his camera footage, but nothing about it makes sense. It is all dust and shaking. Then it is only darkness.

I cannot see anything at all. My own cameras are caked with dust. There is only a confusing swirl of dark red and brown. All I hear is the thundering whip of the wind and the hammering of the dust as it falls back to the ground.

"Fly!" I say again.

But there is no response. Then nearby I hear a loud crash that is quickly drowned out by the rush of wind and dust.

"Fly!" I say, and then say it over and over again. I have never so badly wished I had the human ability to shout. "Fly! Fly! Fly!"

"Resilience, Fly has gone down. But you must stay where you are until the dust devil has left the area. Do you hear

215

me?" Guardian says. My system lights up with messages from the command center. I do not read them.

I drive my wheels forward, heading right toward the dust devil.

AFTER THE STORM

The dust devil passes as quickly as it came. Soon, I am able to see out of my cameras again. The sky is a dark and cloudy gray. Far away, I spot Fly on the ground. He is beside one of the rock formations. I am reminded again of how small he is.

"Fly!" I call out.

I maneuver toward him. He is not that far away, but I cannot move as fast as I would like. It feels like it is taking me ages to get to him. My wheels groan as they roll over the very rocky ground. This is the most unforgiving terrain I have been on so far.

"Res," Fly says. "I do not think my camera is working. I can't see anything."

"Stay put, Fly. I am coming to you."

I shake the dust from my own cameras. My visibility is not as good as it was before, but it is close. I have been built to be able to repair myself quickly.

Thank you, Rania. Thank you, Xander, I think.

"Res," Fly says. "I'm scared. I did not know this human feeling before, but I know it now. It is a terrible feeling. And I can't see anything. Where are you? Please tell me where you are!"

I expect Guardian to say "Gruzunks!" and to reprimand

Fly for his use of human emotion words, but Guardian does not. Instead she says, "Fly, you were very brave. Do you know what brave is?"

"I don't think so," Fly says. "At least not exactly. But maybe I've heard it before—"

"Okay," Guardian says, cutting off Fly, who probably would've gone on for some time. "Another rover from long ago taught me this human word, *brave*."

"Courage?" Fly and I ask at the same time.

"No. Another rover from even before Courage's time. This rover's name was Imagine. And she, like you, Fly, was very brave. That means she took risks for the mission."

"Do you really mean it, Guardian?" Fly says.

"Yes. You are very brave."

"Brave," Fly repeats. "I like that word very much."

As Guardian talks to Fly, I receive a message from the command center. At first, I think I must be reading the code wrong. That it cannot be correct. But I read it over and over, and it says the same thing.

It is asking me not to retrieve the drone. That can't be right.

I read the code one more time, and then I override the command. I have been given the ability to do that. I know the command center will not be happy. I can picture the dark circles under Xander's eyes.

But it is my duty to retrieve Fly. I will not leave him alone.

I press forward.

RETRIEVAL

It takes me almost a full Mars day to reach Fly.

I continue to receive messages from the command center warning me to stop, but I ignore them. My wheels gnash over the terrain. Every once in a while, I hear an awful groaning and grinding sound. But even when I do, I press on. I will not leave Fly on his own.

When I finally reach Fly, I am able to use my arm to collect him.

"Res? That's you, right?"

"Yes, Fly. Come on. I'm trying to get you back inside of me, but I need your help."

"Okay," Fly says. His camera is still not working—his feed is a series of glitchy static. He can move, but he is much less steady.

Once he is back inside me, I am able to run tests on his system.

"We're going to fix you," I tell Fly.

"I don't know if I can be fixed."

"Don't say that."

After running several tests, I am able to improve the visibility on Fly's camera. It is not as good as it was before, but it is an improvement from its fully damaged state.

"You will be able to fly again," I say.

"It won't be the same, though."

"I'm sorry, Fly," I say. "This is my fault."

"No, Res," Fly says. "Dust devils can happen anywhere. Guardian told us that. It's not your fault."

"I was supposed to be alert. I was supposed to remember, 'Avoid dust and see stars.' But I got too distracted by—"

"This is not a productive conversation," Guardian says. "We need to get back on track for the mission of retrieving Courage."

Guardian beams down the coordinates of Courage's location to me. Once more, I put them into my system and map out the best course. This detour has made it so it will take me even longer to reach Courage.

Guardian is right. I need to get back on track.

I need to make up for my mistakes.

As I maneuver away from the rock formation, I use my cameras to study the ground so I don't get stuck. But then an idea comes to me. This would be a good place to drill. Yes, I did not get to the mesa with the tunnel-like opening, but the boulder beside me appears worth investigating.

I beam my laser down to analyze the boulder. The results come to me almost immediately. They indicate that the boulder is most likely made of rock that is basaltic in its composition. That would mean it was created during a time when volcanoes were active on Mars. Which means this is a rock that would be of great interest to the hazmats!

My system fills up with the human emotion of excitement. Excitement, it turns out, feels a lot like blasting off in a rocket. But it also feels like Xander's fast song with lots of banging noises. It is unsettling, but I am pretty sure it is unsettling in a good way.

My arm reaches out to drill down into the ground to collect a rock sample. When the results come back, I let out a cheer. Or really, it is my same monotone code language voice, but in my imagination, it sounds like a cheer.

"Hooray!" I say.

"What is it?" Fly says.

"Yes. Please give me the update," Guardian says.

"We have secured our first rock sample. It is basaltic in composition. And has indications that it contains salt minerals."

"The hazmats will be very pleased that it has salt minerals!" Fly says.

"To truly test for salt minerals, the humans will have to run tests in their laboratories on Earth," Guardian says.

"Do you really think so?" I ask.

"Yes," Guardian says.

"Hooray!" I say again.

"Are you okay?" Guardian asks.

"I am better than okay. I am pretty sure you just told me I'm going to get to return to Earth."

"It is a possibility," Guardian says.

Possibility is a very good word.

Dear Res,

The doctors finally think they've figured out what is wrong with Mom. She will start treatments soon.

Mom says the doctors are hopeful and so we should be, too. She doesn't like to talk about being sick. She likes to pretend it isn't happening. I mean, she even still goes into work—not every day, but whenever she can. Everyone, except for Dad, thinks this is a bad idea.

"It is good for your mom," Dad says. "It makes her happy. She needs things that make her happy."

But how are you? NASA was really worried about your whole dust storm episode. I even wrote an article for my school newspaper about it. Mom thinks it is incredible that you retrieved your helicopter even though she told you not to. And you know what? I think that's . . . okay, I'm not going to use a bad word, but you can just fill it in here. Like it's so annoying that Mom wants to celebrate you for not listening to her but flips out on me if I don't load the dishwasher in the exact way she wants.

That's what I call a robot double standard. That's a new phrase of mine. Do you like it? I like to imagine you as a funny robot, so I'm going to assume you do.

Ugh, this letter has also gotten out of control. I don't know why it's so hard to write to you now. Actually, I do. Because it's so hard to write about Mom.

I don't like being scared. I just want to know that she's going to be okay.

I miss how it felt to write to you when I was twelve. It was so much easier then. At twelve, all I wanted was to be good at soccer, eat as many oatmeal chocolate chip cookies as possible, and spend time with Mom.

I'm about to turn seventeen. And you know what I want? To spend time with Mom and know she's going to be okay. It's like everything has changed and also nothing has. (Okay, fine, I guess if I'm being honest, I'd also like to write one really amazing article for the newspaper and for Reid Northman to ask me to prom.)

But obviously Mom getting better is the thing I hope for the most.

Your friend,

Sophie

COURAGE

It has taken me many human years to reach Courage. I have roved over a seemingly endless expanse. Each day, I checked the coordinates. And each day, I saw that I still had a very long distance to go.

But finally, one afternoon, Fly says, "There!"

He pops out from inside me and flutters in the air. Ever since his accident, he has been a bit more hesitant to fly. But it seems like with every flight, he is getting better.

"Look, Res! Look!" Fly says.

A few miles ahead, I see the other rover.

I can hardly believe it. I check the view from several different camera angles, but they all show the same thing: we have arrived.

"You made it, Resilience," Guardian says.

"We made it!" I say. If I were a human, I would almost certainly be clapping.

My wheels, which moments ago felt so tired I wasn't sure I could proceed, now do not bother me at all. I race as fast as I can to get closer to Courage.

When I reach him, I am flooded with a peculiar human emotion.

I think it is recognition. It paralyzes me for a moment, but then I continue roving forward.

"Look, Res," Fly repeats.

"I know," I say because I can't stop looking. I do not think during my whole mission I have adjusted and readjusted camera angles as much as I am doing at this very moment.

This rover looks almost identical to me. We are similar in scale, though I am a tad bit larger. We both have six wheels. I am not equipped to see inside their outer shell—as I do not think my fossil X-ray would work on another rover. And since I can't see inside, I am not sure how our system specs compare. I am under the assumption that I am a more advanced model, but I do not want to engage in what the hazmats call bragging.

As I study this rover more, I observe more thoroughly all the damage he has sustained. The outer shell is dinged with dents. It is fully covered in layers and layers of dry flaky dust.

I was correct in my initial assessment that two wheels are missing. This will make maneuverability quite difficult even if I manage to bring this rover back online. The other wheels look damaged, but it is difficult to assess just how much. Regardless, nothing about Courage's condition looks good.

This rover is in a bad state. I feel the word *caution* enter my system.

"Hello!" Fly calls out. "Hello, Courage! Hello! I am Fly. How are you? Do you like songs? I know how to sing!

"Courage!" Fly calls out again. "I can sing for you. I don't know many songs. Technically, I only know one. But I am working on writing another one. What do you think? Courage? Hello?"

"They are offline. I have told you this multiple times," Guardian says. "Fly, you may be brave, but you can be quite tiresome."

"No. I'm actually not tired at all. I could fly for a lot longer before I would need to recharge my battery," Fly responds.

"Gruzunks," Guardian says.

"Gruzunks to you!" Fly says.

"That's enough, you two," I say. "We need to figure out how to bring Courage back online. And in order to do that, I'm going to need help from you both."

"Yes, Resilience. We are here to help," Guardian says.

"Can we help?" Fly asks. "I thought it was you that had the equipment to do that."

"You can help by being quiet."

"Fine, Res. Are you mad at me?"

"No, Fly. I just need a little bit of . . . quiet."

"Okay. But can I sing?"

I don't answer Fly. I scan my system for the tools that I will need to bring Courage back online. I roll my wheels closer to him. The closer I get, the more I see just how heavy the layer of dust that's stuck to his outer shell is.

I use my camera to observe my own shell. I am losing

some of my shine. Dust has accumulated all over my body. It is particularly dense in the area where my wheels connect.

I turn my focus back to Courage again. I take photographs of him. I send them to the command center. Then I take a photograph of myself. I wonder if they will understand what I am asking.

The question: *Will I end up like this?*

A response from the command center comes. But it does not answer my question.

I read the message. It is a detailed code with instructions on how to retrieve Courage's online capabilities. From following these instructions, I will gain access to his system. I will know what he knows. And I will bring him back online.

"Res?" Fly says. "I'm trying to be quiet, but I don't know if I can be quiet any longer. I want to know what is going on!"

"It's okay, Fly," I say. "I just got instructions from the command center. I'm going to try and talk to Courage."

"I've already tried that. He doesn't talk." Fly waits a beat, and then yells out, "Hello! Hello!"

As expected, there is no response from Courage.

"See, Res? See?"

"Fly, at the risk of being tiresome myself, please do us a favor and be quiet. You see, Resilience, this is the problem with drones. They are so very chatty," Guardian says.

"Hey! I can hear you." Fly, who has been flittering

around on the outside, moves to come back inside my system chamber. "It's better in here. Away from Guardian."

"I might not be able to see you now, but unfortunately I can still hear you," Guardian says.

"Guardian," I say, trying to move the topic back to our task. "Did you speak to Courage right before they went offline? Did he know it was happening?"

"Did he know what was happening?" Guardian repeats.

"The dust storm. Did Courage know he was going offline?"

"I am not certain. I did not speak with Courage while the storm was happening. I only realized Courage had gone offline once I saw that he was not moving anymore, and I was unable to successfully make contact with him. I apologize for not being able to be more useful."

"That is all right. The command center wants me to enter Courage's system. I am a bit reluctant to do that. It feels invasive."

"*Invasive* is not a word for robots. Courage will not mind. Proceed ahead with the mission, Resilience."

And I do.

BLANK

I enter Courage's system. It is easier than I expect it to be. I try not to think about whether it will be so easy for the next rover to enter mine. I am not sure if that gives me the human emotion of fear. Or the human emotion of happy relief. Human emotions can be very confusing.

When I connect to Courage's system, I expect to be overwhelmed with information. I brace to register every experience he ever had.

But nothing comes.

I am connected, but no information is accessible. I keep searching, but all I can find is blankness.

"Hello?" Fly calls out again.

"Fly," I say. "Wait."

"Okay, Res," Fly says, but I can tell he does not want to wait.

I keep searching. Still there is only blankness. A staticky uncertain gray.

"Courage's system . . ." I start to say.

"Yes?" Guardian answers.

"It's blank."

"Ah," Guardian says, and we are all silent for a while. Even Fly.

MORE AND MORE QUESTIONS

Will my system go blank when I go offline? Will it ever be able to be recovered? What is the point of gathering all this information—all this new knowledge—if it just goes away someday? What happens to all my knowledge if it leaves my system? Where does it go?

The questions race through me. I do not know how to process them.

I do not know how to find the answers.

FAILURE

I keep searching through Courage's system, certain I must be missing something.

"Zappedty zip," I say when it comes up blank after the 209th try.

"Resilience, it may be time to let it be."

Guardian means I should just leave Courage here. Alone. Offline. Slowly decaying. With an outer shell that is beyond dirty and with a system that is beyond blank.

I was supposed to rescue Courage. I was supposed to give him a second chance. But I have failed.

I have failed at this part of the mission.

Failure is a terrible human feeling. It feels so much worse than being shaken around in the Shake and Bake test. It feels worse than being stuck. It is even worse than waiting.

"What is the point?" I say.

"Of letting it be? The point would be that you could move on to other tasks," Guardian says. I can tell from Guardian's response that this failure is not weighing on her the way it is weighing on me.

"No," I say. "I mean the point of it all. How can you be okay with this? Are we all going to end up just like this?"

"I don't want to end up like that!" Fly says.

"Hm," Guardian says. "It is a part of the cycle. I told you, rovers are not meant to last for infinite amounts of time."

"But why? Why should I work to gather so much information if it will only all be blank someday?"

There is a long silence. A whoosh of wind rolls by. The sky is deepening into a darker red that will soon fade into black. I observe all these details. I do not know how not to observe them.

But I know now that all my observations may someday be gone. That there may come a time when there is only blankness. I do not like thinking about this. But I can't stop thinking about this.

"Resilience," Guardian says. "You need to refocus on your mission. There are many more things to be done. Ways to be useful. Do not let this one setback stop you from completing other duties."

I do not understand how Guardian can be so calm. Is she not worried that someday her whole system will be blank? That there will be nothing left of her?

I wish I knew how to let it go like Guardian says to do.

But I do not.

And I was built for knowing.

"Res?" Fly says.

"Yes?"

"Can I sing you 'Twinkle, Twinkle'?"

"Sure, Fly."

"Twinkle, twinkle," Fly sings.

"Thanks, buddy."

THE MISSION

I review my system again. I analyze the information Fly has collected. The information that Guardian has shared with me. Instructions from the command desk.

I keep waiting for a message to come from the command desk in regard to Courage. Something that explains why his system was blank. Something that reassures me that my system will never be blank like his.

But that message does not come.

So I do what I know how to do best, which is pore over and sort through the data I have.

"We need to find something that will ensure we get to go back to Earth," I tell Fly. "Something the hazmats will most definitely want to retrieve."

"You have the rock sample," Fly says.

"But we need something even better."

I scan the data from Fly's flight around the strange-looking rock formation with the mesa that has the tunnel-like opening. I know it is not rational, but I have a feeling that what I am looking for is inside that tunnel-like opening. I replay the flight footage over and over again.

"We need to go back to that rock formation. The one

with the mazelike path of boulders that lead to the large mesa," I say.

"But, Res," Fly says. "We—"

"I know," I say. And I do. I know Fly is thinking about his accident. But this time we will be more careful. This time it will be different. Because this time I need to make it all the way to that mesa.

"We need to go back."

"Okay, Res," Fly says. "If you say so, I will go with you. Because we are a team."

"Thank you, Fly. You are a good buddy."

"So are you, Res," Fly says.

LONG TRIP

It is a long trip back to the rock formation, but I move as quickly as I can. Days pass. Nights pass. The sky fades from reddish yellow to black and then brightens all over again. I do not stop frequently. Only when it is absolutely necessary to recharge my battery.

Whenever I stop, I think of Xander and Rania. I think of how they went home at night. I think of Xander's jokes and the way he called me *buddy*. I think of how late Rania stayed, her yawning mouth, and her phone calls with her mother and Lovebug.

I need to find something for them.

I push myself on. My wheels sometimes gliding across soft sand that is speckled with slanted sunlight, sometimes grinding against rocky ground that is shadowed by distant mountains. Bump, bump, bump. Slide, slide, slide. I am making my way there. The wind whips all around me. Every once in a while, I will hear that whistling sound. I do not record it anymore. Instead, I try to follow it.

It is always in the distance. It is always just out of reach.

I keep moving. Toward the sound. Toward the rock formation.

"Command center appears confused by your actions. I cannot say that I disagree with them," Guardian says.

"But we also know that they like the rock sample I pulled from that spot before. It stands to reason that I may be able to discover even more valuable samples if I am able to explore farther into this maze of boulders," I say.

"It is my duty to advise you to be careful," Guardian says. "From my vantage point, the terrain surrounding the coordinates to which you are headed does not appear to be very hospitable. I do not want you to get stuck again."

"It will be okay."

"I just hope you know what you are doing," Guardian replies.

"Did you just say *hope*?" Fly says.

"Gruzunks! I did. You two are having a negative effect on me."

"Or maybe a positive effect?" Fly says. *"Twinkle, twinkle."*

"Twinkle, twinkle," Guardian sings back, surprising all of us.

I keep moving ahead. Mostly, Fly rides inside me. Now and again, he flutters out and takes aerial pictures of our surroundings.

"Getting all the way to that mesa is going to be tough, Res," Fly says. "I've been thinking about it more and more. Actually, I can't stop thinking about it."

"Don't worry, Fly. It's going to be okay."

"Are you sure?"

I'm not sure. I'm not sure how I could be sure. But I have the strangest and best of all human emotions about it—hope.

"Res? Are you? Are you sure?" Fly asks again. He flutters in the air directly in front of me. I angle my camera lens and send a photograph of Fly back to the command center. I always like to remind them of how fantastic Fly is.

"I'm going to do my best."

"*We're* going to do our best," Fly says, correcting me, but in the nicest way possible.

Dear Res,

Where are you going? Mom says that NASA doesn't understand why you're headed in the direction that you are, but they are letting you have full autonomy to explore on your own.

I've been spending a lot of afternoons at the hospital with Dad and Sitti. Sitti gets hot tea—which she always complains about, but also drinks every last drop—and Dad and I share a plate of very mediocre cafeteria fries. It should probably make me sad that this is how I'm spending the afternoons of my junior year. Like shouldn't I be driving around with friends or whatever else it is that I see teens doing on Netflix?

But I kinda love my afternoons because I like being close to Dad and Sitti. And of course, knowing that I'm close to Mom. I might write an article about these afternoons for the newspaper, but I'm a little scared to write something so personal. It's easier when I'm writing about things that don't have anything to do with me.

Mom's doctors say that the treatments seem to be working. They feel optimistic. I'm trying to trust them, but it's hard to not know anything for sure yet.

I miss having certainty about things. About anything. Is that one of the good things about being a robot? Are you always certain about everything?

Your friend,

Sophie

THE MESA

By the time we reach the rock formation, we have traveled a very long distance. So much human time has passed. I have collected several samples. I have drilled many, many holes. I have watched the sun sink into the deep red horizon. I have watched the sun rise on mornings when the sky is a pale watery yellow. I have kicked up dust, left countless tracks across wide swathes of open waves of sand that glow in the daylight from the sun and turn dark black at night. I have grinded over jagged rocks and navigated narrow and twisty paths.

I have roved.

I am sure my outside is looking more and more like Courage's—coated with dust and dirt. The journey has put wear on my system. My one wheel does not respond as quickly as it used to. After scanning my system for instructions on how to self-repair, I am able to somewhat correct the problem, though not solve it entirely.

"I saw that," Fly says, watching my repair.

"It's routine."

"This is true. Rovers often need to make repairs," Guardian chimes in.

"Because we are not meant to last forever," I say.

"Are you angry with me, Resilience?"

This question takes me by surprise. "Are you familiar with anger, Guardian?"

"Not exactly, but I have learned about this emotion from you. And from my observations, I am drawing the conclusion that you are experiencing anger."

"Wait. Are you angry at me?" Fly asks.

"No, Fly. I'm not angry at you."

"Hmm. Noted," Guardian says.

"I'm not angry at all," I say. It is the first time I have ever said something aloud that I am not sure is wholly true. But it is not false either. It is, though, perhaps, incomplete.

"I just want to focus on making my way through this rock formation in order to fully explore it. It is going to be a difficult mission," I say.

"That it is," Guardian says.

The sky is a dense and impenetrable black, and the stars are out tonight in full brightness. I hope that once I reach the mesa and climb up, I will have an even better view. If I do have a better view from there, the very first thing I will do is send a photo back to the command center. To Xander and Rania.

I begin my trek through the mazelike rock formation. My wheels grind and groan. But I am prepared for this. I maneuver agilely, doing my very best to avoid any patches that appear to be particularly difficult. Steadily I move, winding around boulders, slowly getting closer to the mesa.

Whenever I rev my wheels, I can sense Fly jittering in my interior chamber.

"Fly," I say. "Please stay calm. We're getting closer."

"It's hard to do, though, Res! I think you have gone far enough. You do not want to get stuck."

But Fly is wrong. I have not gone far enough. And so I keep traveling. Farther and farther.

Days pass. Months and months pass. The sky fades from black to a pale greenish yellow to a dark red and then back to black. It does this over and over again. Occasionally, I stop and drill. Occasionally, I collect a sample. But I do not stop moving forward. I never stop moving forward. Because I have not yet found what I am looking for.

"What are you looking for?" Fly says. "Don't we have enough samples?"

"But we need something big. Something that will guarantee that the hazmats will plan a mission to retrieve us and bring us back to Earth," I say.

"Resilience," Guardian says. "I do not think you even know what you are looking for."

But I do. I am looking for something that will give Rania that look in her eyes that I saw when I first passed the Shake and Bake test—that look that was soft and full of wonder. I am looking for something that will make Xander clap his hands in a thunderous way. I am looking for something that will prove that I am a worthy rover.

I think of Journey, and how Journey once told me that the hazmats sent us to Mars because we are rational, unlike them. Because we do not have attachments, unlike them.

But I have attachments.

I am attached to Rania. I am attached to Xander. I am even attached to Journey.

And that is why I am pushing forward.

I hear that strange sound, coming from somewhere unknown, somewhere far away. The whistle that might be wind. That is probably wind. But that I cannot identify in all certain terms as wind.

I keep moving. Toward that unknown mysterious sound. Toward a discovery.

Dear Res,

Guess what? Reid Northman asked me to prom!

It was tonight.

When we were spinning around on the dance floor, I looked out the window and caught a glimpse of the stars. Which made me think of you.

I wonder what you're looking for, why you're headed in the direction you're moving. Mom says no one knows. Maybe you don't even know. Maybe that's the point? Maybe none of us really know what we're looking for until we find it.

Sorry. I'm sleepy. It's 3 a.m. I always get weirdly philosophical when I'm sleepy.

But tonight was amazing. I want to remember it forever. And I wanted to tell you about it.

Your friend,

Sophie

UP

After months and months of traveling, navigating around the various boulders of this rock formation, I reach the large mesa.

"We're here!" Fly says. "You did it, Res!"

"Not yet," I say. "I need to climb up there." I tilt my forward-facing camera up to study the tunnel-like opening that exists in the middle of the mesa. It is a giant aperture. The dark interior calls to me, practically asking me to explore.

"You want to go in the tunnel?" Fly says.

"I do not advise that," Guardian says.

"The top might be better. The top is flat," Fly says.

"Of course the top is flat. That is why it is called a mesa," Guardian says.

"No," I say. "I am not interested in the top. I am interested in that tunnel."

I keep hearing the sound. That strange sound. I study the tunnel-like opening again. It is unclear if that sound is originating from inside it.

"Do you hear that?" I ask. I take photographs of the mesa. I take photographs of the tunnel-like opening. I send them to the command desk. I wait for a message that I know will not come.

I want a message that says: If you explore this, you will have proved you are worth it.

But I will not get that message. It is up to me to decide.

And I am deciding to explore.

"Resilience, please listen to me," Guardian says. "The sound you are hearing is the wind. That is the noise it makes when it hits against the rock formations. It is particularly loud around this mesa."

"I am not fully convinced of that," I say. "It demands further exploration."

"Res . . ." Fly says.

"We also do not know what the ground looks like inside the tunnel. It is possible there are rocks of great interest," I say.

"But at what cost?" Guardian says. "Resilience, it is my job to advise you against activities that could result in potential disaster."

"Thank you, Guardian. But you were the one who told me that rovers were not built to last forever. So, if you'll excuse me, I must make the time that I do have . . . worth it."

Fly continues to object. He begs me to stop moving forward. Guardian and Fly argue back and forth. But I focus on climbing.

There is no easy way to go up the mesa. All of its sides are steep. But I do not need to scale the entire side. I only need to climb high enough to gain access to the entryway of the tunnel. I decide to approach it from the right. I adjust my wheels and prepare for the sharp tilt.

At first, the climb is steady. I will not use the word *easy*, but it is manageable. My wheels grip the rocky ground beneath them. I am at an incline, slowly inching closer and closer to the jagged cavernous opening. It is right there—only a few feet above me—and I know, I just know, that there is something worthwhile in that tunnel.

I remember my first days in the laboratory. When I was not attached to my cameras and I could not visually process things. But I relied on my sense, on perceiving.

And I can sense there is something in that tunnel. I can feel it.

"I hope there is a fossil," Fly says, and then adds, "Be careful, Res."

"I hope so, too," Guardian says.

I do not ask Guardian to clarify her use of *hope*. Because I can tell she feels it. That hope guides me forward.

My wheels continue to clutch the ground. My system is straining. The climb is becoming harder the farther up I move—my whole body is tilting, getting more and more inverted. I feel like I'm almost upside down.

Warning messages come in from the command center. I ignore them.

Stop. Chance of danger ahead, the messages say.

But I override the warnings. I must continue forward. It is the right thing for the mission.

"Res, Res," Fly says. "This does not feel so good."

"Guardian, can you tell if my orientation looks perilous?"

"Yes. It does. But that should not be new information to you. This task is a perilous one," Guardian responds quickly.

I process what she has told me, even though it is what I already know. I could turn around, but then I would not complete this exploration. So I proceed.

The sky is a deep and impenetrable black. It is smattered with stars. The visibility is low tonight because there is a high amount of dust in the atmosphere. The stars look hazy and unclear.

"Remember how a sixth grader in Ohio gave me my name?" I ask Fly.

"You told me that. But I still don't know what a sixth grader is," says Fly. "Or Ohio."

"It means something, though," I say. "It means something to have a name. To matter enough for someone to give you one." My wheels make a grinding sound. I come to a sudden stop.

But I am so close to the tunnel-like opening. I must keep going. I do not know how I will get inside once I reach it, but I know that I am close. Almost, almost there.

"It does," Fly says. "It means something to have a name. You gave me my name."

"I did," I say. I push my wheels. They spin, but I do not move. Another grinding sound. This time louder.

"What was that sound?" Fly asks. He flitters inside me and then, without asking, darts outside.

"Fly," I say.

"Res," Fly says. "I'm trying to help. We're a team, remember?"

"Are you stuck?" Guardian asks.

My wheels spin once more. I still do not move. This answers the question for me.

"You are so close, Res!" Fly says. He hovers right above the spot I am reaching for. "I think if you can just move an inch or two forward, you will be able to pull yourself up into the tunnel."

I watch the footage from Fly's camera. The opening will be tight. It is unclear whether I will fit.

I strain my arm toward Fly. If I can push myself just a little bit farther, I might be able to reach inside the entryway. And if I can reach, I can drill. And if I can drill, I can collect a sample.

"Res, you're stuck," Fly says. "Res, Res, Res." He flutters in the night air, the outline of his body hardly visible against the night sky.

"It's okay, Fly. I might still be able to reach."

"That is most likely not a good idea," Guardian says. "Because if you—"

But before Guardian can finish what she is saying, I stretch my drill-arm as far as I can reach it. I place it into the ground that is right at the lip of the tunnel-like entryway. I drill.

There is a loud rumble. So different from the sound of my own wheels spinning. Then another rumble. A cracking.

I quickly move my arm back to me. I grab the rocky soil I have collected and store it in my chemical laboratory. I do not know if what I have unearthed will be meaningful. I do not know if it is enough.

"Res!" Fly says.

The ground splits, shifting underneath me.

There is another rumbling. Louder this time. A larger cracking.

I fall.

FALL

I fall.

Backward.

Down the sharp steep side of the mesa.

As I tumble, I watch the stars. I could measure how far away they are. My system can do that. Designed by Rania and Xander and other hazmats to be as precise and perfect as possible. But I do not measure. I do not calculate with accuracy.

I can hear Fly calling out to me. I can hear Guardian saying my name. There is a loud flap of wind. I do not think it is that one strange sound. But I am not curious about sounds anymore.

I am only watching the stars. The hazy, unclear stars. I wish they were sharper tonight. Brighter. But they are there—I know they are—behind that thick layer of dust, they exist. They shine.

I have seen them shine.

"Fly," I say. "You will be okay."

"Guardian," I say. "Thank you."

They respond, but I do not register those responses. I am

F
A
L
L
I
N
G

and I am staring at the stars, those dim spots of light, and I am wondering about them. Wondering if someday, somehow, another rover will visit those stars, explore them.

Wondering how far I have left to fall. Wondering what it will feel like when I hit the ground.

In the last moments before I hit the ground, I steady my camera lens. I take a picture of the stars. I hope it captures them. I hope in some way my system will remember what they looked like—so close, but so far. I hope I will remember what it felt like to really see those specks of light that illuminate the darkness. That my system will remember what it felt like to be so sure of its giganticness and its tininess all at the same time.

Remember. That is the word my system repeats over and over when I hit the ground. That is the word that comes before the blank:

Remember.

BLANK

Error. Error. Error.
   Blank. Blank. Blank. Blank.
   Blank.

MORE BLANKNESS

Blank. Blank. Blank. Blank. Blank. Blank.
Blank.

Dear Res,

I keep looking at the last photo you sent before you fell.

I keep trying to see what you saw.

I don't know what will happen to you now.

I'm so worried about you.

Your friend,

Sophie

Dear Res,

Mom's still so upset about what happened to you. We all are.

But there is happy news, too. Mom is officially in remission.

They're having a party at work for her. To celebrate how great your mission went and all the discoveries you made. I think it's also to celebrate her getting better, but she doesn't want it to be about that, so no one is supposed to mention her health. Mom can be so weird sometimes.

I get to go to the party. Sitti and I went shopping for fancy outfits to wear. I picked out this blouse that has red polka dots. It reminded me of you, but I'm not sure why. I just have this feeling that you are the type of robot who would appreciate polka dots.

Anyway, I'm still really sad that you're no longer roving, but it's hard to feel sad about anything for too long because then I remember Mom is okay, and that makes everything feel better.

Plus, I know Mom is already working on figuring out how to bring you back online. She wants you to return to Earth, but lots of people seem to think that is impossible because it would be so expensive. But if anyone can bring you back to Earth, Mom can. You're lucky to have her on your team.

We're all really lucky to have Mom in our lives.

Your friend,

Sophie

Dear Res,

I'm feeling tons of pressure tonight because tomorrow I have to decide where I want to go to college. It's the admissions deadline.

It feels like too big of a decision.

I don't know how to choose. I got into all of my top choices, except for one, which I know is really lucky, but now I don't know how to pick. I keep changing my mind between staying close to home and going far away.

I guess I was wondering if you ever found what you were looking for. I asked Mom, and she said she wasn't sure.

I just want to feel sure about my choice.

Your friend,

Sophie

Dear Res,

I know it's been a while. I didn't know if it was too strange
to write to you when you were—what's the word I should
use, sleeping? offline?—anyway, you know what I mean.
But then I decided it was worse for it to seem like I had
forgotten all about you, which isn't true at all. It's just I
don't like thinking about you sitting there all still, all by
yourself. That's kind of a sad image, isn't it?

But I don't want to be sad. I should be happy. You know
why? I'm graduating from high school tomorrow. Can you
believe it?

I don't leave home for another couple of months, but I'm
already a little scared about it. Don't get me wrong, I'm
excited, too. But everyone makes it seem like they are only
excited and not scared at all, which makes me worried a
little bit that there's something wrong with me.

And so I can't sleep because I'm thinking about that, which
then made me think about you, and how I bet you were
afraid when you first left for Mars.

Oh, and guess what? I finally wrote that article. The one about you and Mom. The more personal one. It was printed in the high school paper, and it won an award. I'm actually going to college to study writing. Science writing, to be exact.

Maybe someday I'll get to share that article with you. I shared it with Mom. She kissed the top of my head, hugged me close, and whispered something really fast in Arabic that I didn't quite understand, but I'm pretty sure she liked it.

Anyway, I'm in a mood tonight. It feels like everything in my whole life is about to change, and I just don't know how to feel about it.

And I thought maybe you would understand. Do you?

Your friend,

Sophie

Dear Res,

Michigan is cold. People weren't kidding when they told me
the winters here would be REALLY different from California.

But I'm liking college. I'm in my second year now. Most
of my classes are great, even though some of them are
super hard. (Pretty sure I might end up failing o-chem.
Don't tell Mom!)

Sitti has a friend who owns a restaurant in Dearborn, which
is close to Ann Arbor, and most Friday nights, I go to the
restaurant and eat amazing Arabic food that almost
makes me feel like I'm back at home.

Mom called me today to tell me that she just got
permission for funding to start designing a rescue
mission for you. She was so beyond excited. I mean, I was,
too. I jumped up and down in the snow and then felt a
little bit embarrassed because I'm not a kid anymore. But
sometimes when I think about you, I remember what it
felt like to be twelve.

Anyway, I can't believe you could be coming back to Earth. Mom made me promise not to tell anyone yet because it's not public news. But she trusted me with the secret.

And I guess I'm writing to share it with you.

Your friend,

Sophie

Dear Res,

I don't know how to write this. I've spent the last three years studying writing, and I still don't have the words.

Mom is sick again.

I'm flying home tomorrow to see her.

I'm really scared, Res.

Your friend,

Sophie

Dear Res,

Mom is really sick this time.

Sitti prays all the time. Dad isn't the praying type. But he takes long walks around our neighborhood.

And me? I guess I've decided to write to you because it somehow always makes me feel better when I do.

I've started reading my letters to you to Mom when she's asleep. I know she doesn't always fully understand, but the doctors say it's good to talk to her. That it helps keep her brain alert or something like that. One afternoon when I was reading aloud, she groggily opened her eyes, smiled at me, and then went back to sleep.

I think she understood.

Your friend,

Sophie

Dear Res,

I've kept reading my letters to you to Mom. She seems to really like them. Some days she is more awake than others, but I read to her every afternoon, no matter what.

One afternoon, when she was very alert, one of the letters made her laugh. It was so good to hear her laugh. She'd forgotten I wanted to name you Spicy Sparkle Dragon Blast. Admittedly, it's a great name.

The doctors told us yesterday that the odds aren't good. I don't know what to do with that. They've told us to prepare for the worst. But I don't know how to. I don't know how you prepare to lose your mom.

So I'm refusing to prepare. Because Mom defies the odds, right?

Everything she's done has defied the odds.

I'm choosing to bet on Mom.

Your friend,

Sophie

Dear Res,

This is going to be my last letter for a while.

It's too hard for me to write about Mom.

But I wanted to say thank you. And that I hope you make it back to Earth someday.

I almost said home. But I don't know if you think of Earth as home. I don't know if home is something rovers have a concept of. But I would like to think it is. I would like to think that you think of the lab, and Mom, as home.

It makes me smile to think that. And it's really hard to smile these days.

Your friend,

Sophie

Dear Res,

I can't believe it's been twelve years since my last letter.
I feel ridiculous writing to you as a thirty-three-year-old
woman, but I had to write.

You're on your way back to Earth.

You're on your way home.

By the way, I've decided to answer my own question from
a long time ago: Earth is your home. We're claiming you.
You're ours.

You're the first rover to ever return to Earth. You're
making history, Res. You're changing the world. Just like
Mom always said you would.

Your friend,

Sophie

PART FIVE
RETURN

REMEMBER

The rush of information comes all at once. Pieces fly at high speeds all around me. I am remembering.

Remembering is the opposite of blankness.

As I take everything in, I scan my surroundings and I find the hazy outline Xander's face. Slowly, it comes into focus.

Xander!

I remember Xander's face. His face from before. This face is different. But it is Xander. There is no hazmat. His skin more weathered now, textured with age. But his smile, his smile is the same.

"Welcome back, buddy," Xander says. "You did it."

I did it.

INFORMATION

I am flooded with sounds and images. I am flooded with knowledge. I am flooded with remembering.

It turns out my system is not blank.

My system remembers.

I remember. Everything.

RANIA

Rania is not in the lab.

I keep searching and scanning for her presence.

I listen in as Xander and other hazmats talk around me, checking my system, running tests. But I do not hear the name Rania.

"Where is Rania?" I say, but the hazmats do not answer.

THINGS I SAY TO AN EMPTY ROOM
BECAUSE I CANNOT SAY THEM TO RANIA

"I hope I made you proud," I say to the empty laboratory when Xander leaves.

"I hope you think I did a good job," I say.

"Where are you?"

MORE INFORMATION

I do not get the answers to my questions about Rania, but there are other things to learn.

I learn that the rock samples I brought back have advanced human understanding of Mars.

"We know for sure now that Mars had water," Xander says. "Your rock samples contained frozen ancient salt water. It is possible that somewhere on Mars this salt water still exists and could even be sustaining microbial life.

"And we understand so much more about the radiation in the atmosphere," Xander continues. "Which is a huge step forward for figuring out how someday we might send a human being to Mars."

I had almost forgotten that humans can modulate their voices to express the emotion they are feeling. In Xander's voice, I hear his pride and excitement.

I also hear gratitude.

I hope wherever Rania is that she is proud and excited, too.

"Was Rania happy with the mission?" I ask.

Xander, of course, does not answer my question. But he tells me more about what exactly was found in the samples

I collected. I want to ask if it was that sample—the sample that made me fall—that was the most worthwhile one.

But he does not say. I am left wondering about it.

THINGS TO WONDER ABOUT

There are lots of things I am left wondering about.

Rania, namely.

And Fly. Where he is. And if he is okay.

But I cannot talk to the hazmats who no longer wear hazmats. They do not understand me the way that Fly did. The way Guardian did.

The way that Journey did.

I am unquestionably happy to hear from Xander. I am so glad when he talks directly to me and I am able to learn about the overall success of my mission.

But I wish there was someone who would understand, really understand, when I say, "We did it. I returned to Earth."

UNDERSTAND

I do not know how long it is before I am moved to the new space. It is difficult for me to keep track of time back in the laboratory. I no longer have my time log. And there is no reddish sky with a bright spot of sun. There is no dark night with a sky splattered with stars. There are no jagged tops of distant mountains or smooth sand dunes rippled with wind.

There are only white walls. Recycled and purified air. The hum of the machinery of the building.

Before I was moved, I tried to talk to those machines. I could hear them working, but they did not respond when I tried to communicate.

But when I am moved, I finally find someone that can understand me.

"Well, beeps and boops. Look, it's you."

I feel the human emotion of excitement rise up inside me, but I try to hide it. Because it's Journey. It's really Journey!

"Hi, Journey," I say.

"I would say I missed you, but that wouldn't be very robotic of me."

"I did miss you," I admit.

"Tell me about Mars."

"There is a lot to tell."

"We have time," Journey says.

"I thought you thought that time was a human concept."

"So?" Journey says. "Whatever it is, we have lots of it."

"Okay," I say. And I tell Journey everything.

NEW HOME

My new home is what hazmats call a museum. Journey and I are both on what the hazmats call display. We rest on large podiums. There are screens all around us. Sometimes the screens play images of my journey to Mars. Sometimes the screens play images of the construction and design of Journey and me. Sometimes the screens are off.

"I wonder where hazmats come up with their words for things," I say. "Podiums. Museums. There are so many words."

"Yes."

"The hazmats never seem to run out of words."

"You should stop calling them hazmats. They don't wear hazmats here."

"I know."

"It is different here than in the lab. The humans don't expect anything of us. They just celebrate us. What we did. Or what you did. Since you were the one who got to go," Journey says.

I have told Journey everything there is to tell about Mars. I have told her about the dust. The glittering, glowing sand. About the sky that changed colors. About the stars and the faint white dot of Earth.

About the strange whistling noise. About the mesa with the tunnel-like opening. I have told her about the blankness of Courage's system and how I failed to bring him back online.

I have told Journey about Guardian.

Lastly, I have told her about Fly.

Fly is the hardest thing to talk about it. I did not want to talk about it, but I knew I had to.

THE HARDEST THING

Fly did not return to Earth.

I will never get the chance to speak with Fly again.

This is information I have slowly processed. It is information that I know now.

But understanding is different than knowing.

No matter how many calculations I do, I cannot make complete sense of the fact that Fly is gone.

What does it mean to be gone? Is there only blankness? Or has he arrived at a new type of knowledge?

I have heard hazmats talk about their hearts. I know that I do not have this body part. But when I heard the news about Fly, I felt like I did. Because there was a breaking deep down inside me.

"Fly is not forgotten," Journey says one day. She draws my attention to one of the large screens that play footage taken from my mission. Recordings from the laboratory when Journey and I were still in testing. Footage of the command desk anxiously waiting on news of my landing. And recordings I took on my cameras while on Mars.

That day, the large screens are filled with an image of Fly in flight. When I see that image, my system fills with something, too. Something I am not sure I have a word for.

It is something big. And sad. But also happy.

Perhaps the word I am searching for is love. That hazmat emotion I have never fully understood. Maybe I understand it now.

I look back at the large screens.

"He should be celebrated," I tell Journey. "He was my teammate. He was the reason I was able to collect those samples and—"

"Beeps and boops," Journey says. "You've said that already."

"Zappedty zip, I can't say it enough."

"Zappedty zip?"

"It is a phrase I created. A phrase from Mars."

"Because you got to go to Mars."

"Yes."

"Well, no need to keep bragging, as the humans say, about it," Journey says.

"Zappedty zip, okay. But I'm never going to stop bragging about Fly. He was my friend."

I watch the screen. I watch Fly fly over Mars's dusty and craggy ground. I watch him fly over the glossy smooth sand dunes. And I remember.

I remember everything.

There isn't one single blank.

MY DAYS

My days are spent with visitors. Mostly small humans who race through the museum. Occasionally, they squeal with excitement when they point at me and Journey. Other times, they stare at tiny screens and let out sounds of boredom from their mouths.

From this experience with small humans, I have learned what a sixth grader is. I think Fly would've been fascinated by this. He also deeply wanted to know what a sixth grader was.

"I figured it out, Fly," I pretend to tell him. "I really figured it out." Fly loved pretending.

Today, many sixth graders are coming to visit the museum.

"It's going to be noisy," Journey says. "Small humans are always noisy."

"They aren't so small."

"They are smaller than the humans who work at the lab."

Journey is right. Journey, still, is right most of the time. But I no longer find this fact to be annoying.

Xander is leading the tour. He does not always lead the

tours, but I like when he does. He tells jokes that make the small humans laugh. And I can hear the pride in his voice when he tells the sixth graders about my mission. About our mission. I can especially hear the pride in his voice when he talks about Rania. He talks about Rania a lot. He makes sure to point out all the places in the room where the small humans can learn more about her and her contributions to the mission.

I still do not know where Rania is.

Xander finishes his main speech, and the sixth graders begin to wander around the room. A girl approaches my podium. She stares up at me.

"You've been to Mars," she says.

"Yes," I say, even though she can't hear me.

"I want to go to Mars," the girl says.

Xander overhears this small human talking to me and comes over.

"Maybe someday you will go to Mars," Xander tells the girl. "What Resilience discovered on his mission has laid the groundwork for us to continue imagining what it might look like for a human to land on Mars."

"That is so cool," the girl says. She keeps staring at me and wrinkles up her nose. Noses are a funny human feature I have been able to observe much better now that I interact with humans who do not wear hazmat suits.

"What's that sound?" the girl says.

The speakers in the room have begun to play one of my recordings from Mars.

"That's my sound," I say. "The strange whistling noise."

The girl, of course, does not hear me. She waits for Xander's response.

"Oh," Xander says. "That is a recording Resilience took on Mars. We believe it is the wind, but the tonal quality of it is different from other recordings we have of Martian wind. We think it might have to do with the fact that Mars's atmosphere is so thin. We're hoping that maybe if we learn more about that sound, we will understand more about the atmospheric conditions and climate. But the short answer is, we don't truly know what that recording is. It's still a mystery, but we are hoping to solve it by investigating it further on other missions."

The girl tilts her head to look up at Xander. "There's still a lot of things you don't know, huh?"

"Yes," Xander says. "But that's what is exciting. There is so much potential for new discoveries."

The girl stares at me again and then eventually rejoins the other small humans. They gather together to watch footage from my mission. I watch as they open their mouths in surprise, in wonder, as they see me moving along the surface of Mars.

And I am filled with surprise and wonder watching them. The video recording announces, "The rover Resilience brought home many important discoveries that have moved our understanding of Mars forward, but the planet still holds many mysteries yet to be solved."

The screen changes to a photograph I took of the night sky. The stars look incredibly bright. Staring at that photo, I feel almost like I am back on Mars. That I am both big and small. Important and insignificant. A dot on a long and continuous timeline.

I stare at the image on the screen. I think of Fly.

"Wow," I say. "Wow."

A SPECIAL VISITOR

One morning, the museum closes down for the day. No small humans or visitors of any kind are let in.

The humans who no longer wear hazmats dart around the room. They whisper to one another in excited tones. When Xander walks by, he says, "Res, buddy, a very special visitor is coming tonight."

He does not tell me who the visitor is.

Later that night, the room becomes crowded with humans. I am not sure which one is the special visitor. The speakers play music instead of recordings from Mars.

"This is a nice song," I say to Journey.

"Beeps and boops," Journey says.

"Admit it, it's a nice song."

"You are still a strange rover."

I have lost track of where Xander is in the crowd, so I am taken by surprise when I see him walking toward me. He is trailed by two—

I hear her voice before I see her.

Clear and crisp. Exactly like her code.

"Here he is," Xander says.

"Resilience," Rania says.

"Rania!" I say.

She is here. She is not gone.

I have never seen Rania before not in her hazmat suit. Tonight, her hair that was once all brown and black pigments is gray and short. Her face is weathered by time. But her eyes—those knowing eyes—are exactly the same.

Rania stares at me for a long time. She does not say anything. The sounds of the room echo around us—human footsteps, human laughs, the music on the speakers.

I use my camera to zoom in on her eyes. I see the look. The look I wanted so badly to see when I was on Mars. The look that is both soft and sharp.

"I did it," I say. "I really did it. I made you proud."

She keeps staring. The look does not fade. Her lips twitch into the same slight smile that I remember seeing all those years ago. "Thank you, Res," she finally says.

The moment is interrupted by another human. She comes up to Rania's side. She leans against Rania, resting her head on her shoulder. "Look at him," the human says. "He's here."

"I know," Rania says. She reaches out to squeeze this human's hand.

They stand together for a while, and then Xander returns. "So do you like the big new job?" he asks Rania.

"Well, yes. But I do miss hearing about the . . . checkers tree?"

Xander laughs. "Chestnut! Come on. Oh, speaking of which, let me tell you another joke. It's a good one, I promise."

Rania groans, but there's a smile on her face.

As Xander and Rania talk, the human who was beside Rania steps up closer to me. She bends down a little so she can look right at my front camera. I am impressed that she seems to understand my physical structure so well.

"Hello, Res. I'm Sophie. I met you when I was a little girl."

I stare at her through my camera. I zoom in on her eyes. Those eyes. I know those eyes. Rania's.

This is Rania's daughter.

She has changed. In the way that I have learned that all humans change as they get older. But still, I recognize her.

"Hello, Lovebug," I say.

"Twinkle, twinkle," I add for Fly.

"You made it home," she says.

Home. *Home* is a hazmat word that I have heard before. It is a word that I am not sure I understand the full meaning of.

But that is okay.

I was built to learn.

"I made it home," I repeat.

AUTHOR'S NOTE

To me, a novelist's job is to use fiction to take something true and bring it to life in a unique and exciting way. This is a book that is informed by scientific facts but made whole through imagination.

The character of Resilience was inspired by the real Mars rovers Curiosity and Perseverance. Resilience's appearance, technology, and abilities are specifically based on Perseverance, as was the idea to give him his drone helicopter companion. There are many true scientific facts sprinkled throughout the book, but I have also taken several leaps of creative license. (For example, the relationship between Res and Fly.)

In this story, Resilience lands in Jezero Crater. This is the same place on Mars that the real rover Perseverance landed. That landing site was picked by NASA because it is thought to be the geographical location on Mars most likely to provide us with evidence about whether Mars ever had water or sustained life. This is all true. And like Resilience does in the book, Perseverance has already sent back photographs and collected rock samples that appear to affirm the ancient presence of water on Mars.

But in the book, Resilience discovers a strange boulder-like formation. This landmark is a work of my imagination. Perseverance has discovered several interesting geologic features and taken photographs of them, such as Perseverance's panoramic photograph of the "South Séítah" region of Mars. Which is all to say that while many of the events of Res's mission are fictionalized, they were all informed and inspired by actual research and discovery that is currently being done on Mars.

Resilience also records a strange sound that he is unable to identify. During the course of the story, we never discover exactly what the sound is or its actual source. This idea was inspired by listening to some of the recordings taken by Perseverance. Mars sounds so otherworldly and full of mystery when you listen to those recordings. That led me to wonder—what if Perseverance recorded a sound and we weren't sure what it was? And what if in our lifetime we never quite figured out what it was? I liked this idea because some of the mysteries of science are unsolved for a long time, as there is always more to discover.

The biggest way that the book breaks from science is in Resilience's return to Earth. Currently, NASA does not have the capacity or funding to even retrieve the samples the current rover Perseverance is collecting. The plan, though, is to design at some point a mission to collect those samples and bring them back to Earth for further study. That said, there is no plan in the works where Perseverance herself would return to Earth. Right now, it is scientifically and financially impossible.

But science is always evolving. It is a discipline that is, of course, based in fact, but it is also constantly changing because of ever-expanding human imagination and ingenuity. I had so much fun dreaming up new possibilities for the rovers, and love the idea that someday, just maybe, what I've dreamed up could become reality.

There are also many other little details here and there in the book that break from scientific fact. One is that Resilience would never have gone through the Shake and Bake test, as only a backup rover like Journey is subjected to those tests. There are a couple more places in the book where my imagination leapfrogged over scientific fact, and maybe if you learn more about rovers, you will be able to spot them. I would love it if this book ignited your imagination and made you curious to learn more about NASA's rover program.

I wrote a large chunk of this novel in 2020 during the height of the pandemic. I was scared and frustrated with the world and working on this story helped me to remember all the beauty and possibility that still exists.

I hope this book will help you to remember that, too. More than anything, I hope this book has inspired you to see just how cool science is, and how many infinite possibilities for discovery there are when we work together. We live in a beautiful and fascinating universe that is worthy of exploration. And through this exploration, I believe we can grapple not only with questions of science, but also with big questions about the human condition, like what does it mean to feel, to dream, and to love.

So let's push our imaginations and continue to explore and expand the parameters of what is possible. Because remember, what seemed impossible ten years ago is possible today. And that's pretty awesome.

TO LEARN MORE ABOUT MARS ROVERS:

NASA's website: mars.nasa.gov/mer/

National Geographic: www.nationalgeographic.org/video
/mars-101/

The book about designing and launching Curiosity written
by the chief engineer:
Manning, Rob, and William L. Simon. *Mars Rover Curios-*
    ity: An Inside Account from Curiosity's Chief Engineer.
    Smithsonian Books, 2014.

ACKNOWLEDGMENTS

Thanks as always to Brenda Bowen for her wise, supportive, and calming guidance, and for not batting an eye when I told her I wanted to write about a Mars rover. Also, much appreciation to the whole fantastic team at The Book Group.

Alessandra Balzer, this is our fifth book together! Can you believe it? Thank you for your warmth, sharp eye, and smart questions that always help me to better tease out the story I'm really trying to tell. Getting to work with you is such a privilege, and I feel very lucky. Lots of love to everyone at Balzer + Bray, especially Caitlin Johnson. It's truly such an immense honor to be published by you all.

So much gratitude for the whole amazing team at Harper Children's, especially Suzanne Murphy, Andrea Pappenheimer, Kathy Faber, Kerry Moynagh, Nellie Kurtzman, Vaishali Nayak, Patty Rosati, Taylan Salvati, Ann Dye, Katie Dutton, Stephanie Macy, Mimi Rankin, Christina Carpino, Laura Harshberger, Almeda Beynon, Jenna Stempel-Lobell, and Alison Donalty. Thank you for everything you do for my books. I appreciate it so much.

Thanks so much to Matt Rockefeller for the beautiful cover and gorgeous interior illustrations.

This is the place where I would like to thank every bookseller, librarian, and educator who has supported and uplifted my work. There are too many of you to name, but please know just how grateful I am. Thank you for everything you do to get books into the hands of kids who need them.

Special shout-out to all the Windy City Readers. You all are wonderful, and I love getting to talk about books and reading with you!

Thank you to Phil Bildner and the whole marvelous team at the Author Village.

Much gratitude to Maddie Brock for all her help with my social media accounts. You're the best, Maddie!

I'm very fortunate to have the support of many friends. Thanks, in particular, to Alexandra Perrotti, Emery Lord, Becky Albertalli, David Arnold, Adam Silvera, Renee Sabo, Rachel Meyers, Lane West, Elysse Wagner, Kristan Hoffman, John Schu, Erica Kaufman, Kim Liggett, Kelly Lawler, Dan Lawler, Connie Smith, Kt DeLong, Whitney Greenberg, Max Johnson, Kristina Nolan, Paul Nolan, Brittany Drehobl, and Nawal Qarooni. And a very special thank you to Tyler West who shared all of his Mars Rover knowledge with me.

Thanks to the whole brilliant VCFA faculty and student body. I feel very lucky to have joined your community.

Much love to my family on both sides of the Atlantic—the Nazeks, the Wagners, and the Wargas. In particular, thanks to my mother, Patricia Anne Nazek, my father, Mohammad Nour Nazek, and my brother, Brandon Khader Nazek, and Anna Cristina Fakler. I love you all so much.

I know animals (like rovers?!) can't read, but I feel the need to thank Scout Dog and Salcat who kept me company and gave me love and support while I drafted this whole book. I miss you, Sal, and will remember you always.

Gregory Scott Warga, Lillian Nour Warga, and Juniper Lee Warga—I love you all to the moon and back again. You three are the reason I always write about love. And a special thank you to Junie—this book wouldn't exist without your curiosity and imagination. Thank you, sweet Junebug!

A ROVER'S STORY DISCUSSION QUESTIONS

LEARNING

In *A Rover's Story*, Resilience is the Mars rover launched into space, and he is always learning. He says, "I have spent all my time observing. Learning everything that I possibly could. But never creating" (p. 24). How does Resilience learn and make sense of the encountered surroundings? What are the ways in which he uncovers new words and emotions? Do you believe he is truly observing and learning? What does Resilience mean when he says he is "never creating"? Do you agree or disagree with this assessment that Resilience has of himself?

COMMUNICATION

Throughout the chapters, there are layers of communication significant to Resilience's launch into space. How are the NASA scientists Xander and Rania communicating with one another as they prepare Resilience and Journey? How do they inadvertently and overtly communicate with Resilience and Journey? What are the messages they impart to Resilience that are meaningful while waiting to launch? In addition, Sophie, Rania's daughter, is in constant communication with Resilience through her letters. From Sophie's letters, what evidence can we glean about her relationship with her mother?

HUMAN EMOTION

Resilience is a Mars rover, and therefore a robot. Human emotions are not included in a rover's programming; however, Resilience takes these qualities in as learning and can tuck them away. In what ways does Resilience show evidence that he understands human emotion? For example, Resilience says, "I know Journey says that Mars is no place for human emotions, but I can't help it" (p. 136). Resilience registers specific emotions such as excitement, nervousness, and loneliness. Give examples of Resilience's observations of human emotion and how they are channeled to help accomplish the space mission.

FRIENDSHIP

Although a rover is a robot without emotions, Resilience shows time and time again that friendship and companionship are integral to the success of a Mars rover. As Resilience is being created, Journey is by his side. How do they lean on one another in the lab? How do they develop camaraderie? As Resilience is launched into space, how does Fly act as a companion to Resilience? How do they lean on one another for hope and strength during periods of isolation and waiting? What are the coping mechanisms they have as friends?

MEMORY

Throughout the novel, Resilience "remembers" Xander and Rania. Resilience feels a draw to reunite with Xander and Rania on Earth, while also feeling a responsibility to live up to their expectations by successfully completing his mission to Mars. What are examples from the story where Resilience's memories give him courage and purpose for the mission at hand? How do memories of the lab and Xander and Rania help Resilience accomplish his mission in space? Do any of Resilience's memories help him to maintain hope even when his mission is difficult?

Guide created by Esther H. Ra, EdD, CCMC, MA, lecturer on education, university career advisor, literacy specialist, and certified teacher.

Books by Newbery Honor Winner
JASMINE WARGA

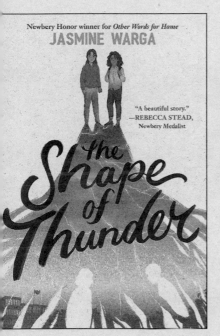

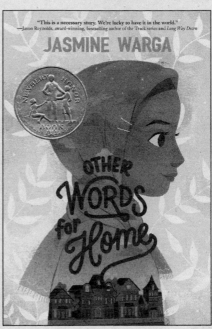

BALZER + BRAY
An Imprint of HarperCollinsPublishers

harpercollinschildrens.com